LOVING *Finley*

LOVING FINLEY

Plump Playwright Act III

With one more hike before winter sets in, Finley can't wait. Hoping to write another romance during those cold months sitting in front of a fire with a tumbler of cognac, she just wants the next few days done and dusted. Except she's on her own. Not that she minds escorting groups of men through the mountains on a 'get-in-touch-with-their-inner-man' camp. She can handle herself and anything her mountain can throw at her. Except this. A flash flood strands her with the sexiest man on the planet. Now she has to get Duke's sexy-as-sin ass to Old Margot's cabin and hope the radio's working.

Dante 'Duke' Delaney, a hotshot baseball player, is fired from the team, yet here he is stuck on a hike he organized. Dealing with their park ranger, a ditzy blonde bombshell with sensual curves, is beyond his tolerance. When a flash floods strands them, what he discovers splinters his assumptions about Fin. She's not ditzy, those curves mask solid muscle, and she's galaxies beyond a bombshell. He wants her, and despite his charm, she resists him. With one taste of her soft lips, he knows, he has just days to convince her to date him.

Also by Sevannah Storm

The Justisaar

*

Inkounter Series

Inkoded

*

Standalones

Xiaxan Fox

Ire of Silver

The Crucible of the Eternal

*

Plump Playwright Series

Plump Jane

Seducing Amelia

Loving Finley

Keeping Tessa

Kissing Navy

Chapter One

Fin giggled as she scrawled across her notebook, capturing her character's sass. "Dude." Still laughing, she snapped the book shut and opened the door. She slid the book under the seat—her hiding place. Alex, her brother, had yet to find her stashes, and just the thought of him reading her erotic stories inflamed her cheeks.

She ducked behind the Ford Bronco to close the dual zip on the last hiking backpack amid the raucous laughter of seven virile men. Each one had appeal: tall, handsome, charming, the-boy-next-door vibe. If she was looking for romance, she might flutter her eyelashes and thrust out her breasts in the hopes of a date.

She snorted. Not after Bryce. Shoving thoughts of her ex-ass aside, she marched to her dad, who kept the group laughing and their enthusiasm levels up. She wanted to be writing, gathering the stories into words and onto paper after she'd spent the season creating them in her mind. Excitement added a bounce to her step. Just one more hike. Drawing a deep breath to fill her lungs with the fragrances of pine and soil, she rubbed her palms down her camo-covered thighs and over curves she hadn't had a year ago. Bryce would have berated her for her extra poundage. He could drown in an alligator-infested swamp for all she cared.

Shyness consumed her like it always did, with an eager crowd, a new day, and a trip up her beloved mountain. She spun on a heel and blew a kiss at the snow-capped shadow covered in pine and oak trees. Time to start the hike. "You got me, big mama?" she whispered, love for her home flooding her chest with warmth and contentment.

Looping her arm around her father's waist, she tossed a beaming smile at the gathered men, praying they didn't notice her blush. This had been her brother's brilliant idea, to lure citified males on a quest to find their inner caveman-lumberjack. His marketing plan had worked with trips booked months in advance.

Investors rolled in. Their interest forced Dad to upgrade their cabins to chalets, driving them from a three to a four-star rating. Hence the renovations he wanted completed before the weather turned.

"Hi, I'm Fin, and I'll be your guide on this trip." She gestured to the row of backpacks. "Choose your color, and we'll get started."

They blinked at her, smirked, or ran their gazes over her figure. Sure, she was short with curves, but her knowledge of the mountain was on par with Dad's. If she was one of her sassy characters, she would shove out a hip, flick her hair aside, and return their grins. Then on a breathy sigh, say how delighted she was to escort them into the dark, dangerous woods. Alas, she wasn't so bold in real life.

"Come now, boys. This isn't my first rodeo, but it is yours." She clapped her hands. "Chop, chop. We have a river to cross."

They hesitated and cast worried glances at her dad. He ignored them and kissed her temple. "Alex is bringing the last of the group. Try to have fun, Finny." He jogged to the Bronco they had shared on the trip up.

Fun? She raised her gaze to the sky. Dark clouds on the horizon hinted at rain past or to come. A wet four days wasn't what she wanted to endure. Glancing at her white T-shirt, she grimaced. Perhaps a change in the uniform might be wise. Chuckling, she imagined her nipples peaking her drenched shirt in the face of seven sex-crazed werewolves. Focusing on the group, she tried to imagine them with fangs and fur. Right, like they would hunt her, exposed nipples or not.

"But, Eli..." A tall, gangly man trailed Dad, a whining twang to his voice.

She ignored their whispered conversation peppered with Whiny-Butt's wild arm swings. The hike wouldn't end if she didn't start it. She had to help the men strap on their chosen backpacks. They grunted and huffed under the awkward weight, their muscles bulging as they adjusted the packs to sit snugly. Their brows furrowed as if the pack meant life or death like they were about to plummet out of a plane.

"What's in these?" a blond grumbled, rolling his shoulders and jarring the backpack. He was cute in a boyish way with plump lips and a crooked nose that added to his charm.

"Everything you'll need to survive without me." She winked. "Not that I'm planning on abandoning you. Unless there's a bear, then we'll sacrifice the slowest."

"You've done this before?" Another man met her gaze, and to his credit, didn't ogle her breasts stretching her T-shirt.

"Every four days. This is the last hike of the season." She bounced around him to help the next man. "Now, I'll learn your names during our time together, but it will help if you say your name when speaking to me."

"Jackson. You do this on your own?" The boyish-blond tugged on his shoulder strap tangled with his T-shirt.

She nudged his hand away to untwist the two, enjoying his sandalwood cologne rising off him. "It varies. Sometimes Dad and I share the role, sometimes my brother and I spend the time together. That's a miracle right there. He's a smart ass." She chuckled. "I love him, though."

"I love you too, sis." Alex smiled, pulling her into a hug. "Go easy on these guys."

Having not heard him pull up, his hug drew a yelp and earned him a poke in the ribs. "I'll try." When he didn't release her, she tapped his shoulders until he let her go, jarring her vision. "Git. Enjoy them strippers." She shoved a roll of one-notes into his hand, wiggling her eyebrows and laughing at his blush.

Alex flipped his blond hair off his temple, looking strange in his dark-blue T-shirt and jeans. The only time she saw him out of his ranger uniform was at family dinners. The same applied to her. They lived and breathed Chibougate Tours. "I plan to. Dad says he's escorting you to Matacona."

Biting her inner cheek, she tried to keep a smile in place. Thanks to Whiny-Butt. That men doubted her abilities was par for the course, still, it stung that her father had caved. The river was half a day's walk, so she shouldn't complain. He could've agreed to do all four days. Tossing her arms around Alex, she hugged and released him, then focused on the task at hand. Whiny-Butt returned and struggled with his backpack. She dipped her chin to her chest to hide a grin; the temptation to let him struggle summoned a delicious bolt of pleasure.

Beside him stood the latecomer.

Mother of parsley. Ice swept through her, raised shivers and goosebumps along her skin, and pebbled her nipples. She hurried to fold her arms across her chest, resisting the urge to look for fangs in the new man's wicked smile. Never had such a reaction gripped her.

Tall, broad-shouldered with brown hair curling over the collar of his black T-shirt stood a man too gorgeous for words. He had a sharp jawline, a wide sensual mouth that added to his sex appeal with the bottom lip pouting a little, and big baby blue eyes like what he had wasn't enough. Mother Nature was a mean-assed...um...cow? Fin winced.

Her heart leapt to choke her, and she scurried to the man on the far right. With the hopes her cheeks would stop burning before she had to speak to the GQ model, she checked each backpack. She bounced on her toes, a little intimidated by the taller men around her. At five-foot-four, she had to accept that God hadn't been generous in that area.

Yet as she worked along the line toward the waiting Adonis, her senses heightened. Every pinch of a strap she adjusted, the burn of a cord she tugged on was made more intense by her nervousness. With a huff at her silliness, she squared her shoulders to face him. What could he do? Sweep her off her feet, toss her over one shoulder, and run through the forest to make wild passionate love to her? Clenching her thighs against the unwanted heat, she pictured her cousin Patrick instead, hoping to calm her ardor. Damn, she missed her bestie. She made a mental note to call him soon.

"Ready?" She scanned the newcomer's backpack, checked where it needed tightening until it rested snug against his back.

He had to bend a little for her to reach the higher buckles. She smiled her thanks but refused to meet his gaze. This close, his spicy cologne tantalized her nose, so she breathed through her mouth. A faint would lead to a canceled hike when all eight men panicked. Giggling, she was tempted to fake it just to see their reactions. The man who prevailed would be the alpha, in control, booming orders, claiming damsels. She shivered with anticipation, despite the dark spot on her heart that had Bryce's fingerprints all over it.

The Adonis was warm, with heat pouring off him, made worse when she stopped an inch from touching him. In her peripheral vision, snapshots of his pecs and bulging biceps burned into her memory banks. Spots circled her vision, and she sucked in a sharp breath. *Get a grip, Finny.*

Whiny-Butt poked his face into her line of sight. "Are you sure you can...?"

Meeting his gaze, she lifted the remaining backpack as if it weighed nothing. She arched her brow at him while she clipped herself in.

"She's sure, Michaels." Adonis grinned, and his dimples shattered her heartrate.

Shaking her head to clear the daze, as if floodlights pinned her to the spot, she skipped to the front and started the hike, aware that the men stared at her thick thighs. And of course, her left butt cheek itched.

Her wider ass hadn't bothered her on previous hikes, but today, with them, she added a little extra sway to her hips as if to say, 'take that.' She leapt to the side of the footpath, careful not to crush too many wilted flowers. Assessing the group, she checked their backpacks sat well and that they followed like ducks in a row. They chatted as if nature wasn't the great silencer. She shrugged. They would soon quieten when the full weight of the packs and the increasing incline affected their ability to breathe.

Alex's disappearing Bronco drew her focus, then she smiled at Dad buckling his backpack on as he hurried to catch up. His wink summoned a smile, and she marched ahead to lead the men again.

Sure, they watched her, and about half of them would flirt with her as the only woman in a ten-mile radius. But, as she'd said, this wasn't her first rodeo, and arrogant men like these led to heartbreak and a minor addiction to pancakes. She huffed. Minor? Now who was she kidding?

Did she long for her days in the city as a girlfriend to a surgeon? Sometimes, but then a crisp breeze would cool the tears on her cheeks and remind her where her broken heart lay. No, she was where she belonged...under the welcoming arms of her mountain.

Chapter Two

Duke hated being late for anything, and this time, his tardiness had inconvenienced the park ranger, Alex, who drove them up a winding road away from the reception. While flexing his stiff fingers that had pinned his phone to his ear for the last fifteen minutes, Duke almost searched for the nefarious device. Thankfully, he had used his curveball throw to smash it against a massive oak towering over the parking lot. His mobile lay in pieces a mile behind him, like his career.

He'd been released permanently and was now a free agent.

'Too old for the team,' his coach had said.

'Make way for fresher, newer talent,' his agent had said.

Neither had said it to his face, choosing to act like cowards and tell him over the phone as if his years of loyalty to the club meant nothing. How many offers from other clubs had he turned down? What a fool he was. He gritted his teeth, trying to contain the fury stiffening his muscles and irritating his ever-present ulcer. He swallowed bile as he fought to calm his ragged breathing.

His teammates waited for him, hoping to enjoy a wilderness retreat. He grimaced and caught Alex tossing him a worried glance as he jerked the SUV to a halt. When the park ranger joined the group, Duke hesitated, choosing to linger for a second, to gain control of his sadness and anger. He clambered out and jogged to where his teammates gathered, summoning his signature smirk. Only to pause.

A curvy blonde bounced around his friends, her glowing smiles and steady chatter not distracting from her deep brown eyes. Her joy, in contrast with his negative emotions, grated on his last nerve, and he raised his pleading gaze to the sky. *Great, this day can't get any worse, can it?*

Her tousled hair was the same color as Alex's, declaring them related, and the way he hugged her confirmed it. Her lush lips and sunscreen-smeared, porcelain skin had no place being here. Vanilla, pine, and mint assailed his senses when she tugged on his backpack's buckles and cords.

He shook his head, not needing this shit, not when his life was falling apart. Sure, he'd heard of the Chibougate Tours and had chosen a hike to evaluate the investment opportunities. He just hadn't realized that a new life was on the horizon, forced upon him regardless of his opinion.

Michaels was being his usual ass-hat self, doubting the woman could lead them. And of course, like the youngest child he was, he whined to her boss...or should Duke say, father? He liked that Chibougate Tours was family-owned and operated. Between the irritation that Michaels was in general and this intense interest in the energetic blonde, Duke would side with the woman.

His defense of her stained her cheeks a delicate pink. As expected, his charm softened the way for him, and if he chose to, he would have her beneath him soon. His well-earned arrogance was a fact. Despite his *advanced* age, he was the playboy of the team.

Not today and not anymore. They were no longer his teammates.

Slapping Jackson on his backpack, Duke trailed their guide and focused on the towering mountain and the winding path climbing toward a roaring river. Anything was better than the sway of her hips and the way her camo pants molded her thighs. She set a steady pace, not once huffing as she paused to describe a green weed or spout the Greek names of trees, which to his unskilled eye looked the same.

Her bright smile and charming chatter accompanied her bobbing pale-blonde curls that formed a halo around her face. Whenever she pointed, her T-shirt pulled tight across her breasts, and when she crouched, the waistband of her pants dipped, revealing the top of her white panties.

He clutched his sweat-saturated chest, testing the thumping, erratic rhythm of his heart. Had she been wearing something a little more sensual, he might have caved and set his sights on her. Serviceable panties said much about her. She was practical. It stood to reason when she led men into the wilds of *her* mountain.

"Did Baxter reach you?" Kensey paused to wipe his forehead on his T-shirt's sleeve. His blond hair was darker than Finley's.

Duke bit his inner cheek, trying to remove thoughts of their guide from his mind. He'd been fired. That should consume his focus for the foreseeable future.

"Yup, before I broke my phone." He shrugged.

"Five minutes. Your filtered water bottles are in the side pouch. Take a moment and rest, but don't forget to let the pine-scented air fill your lungs." Finley's voice traveled far. With a firm nod, she huddled with her father. She tilted her head back and laughed, the sound too husky for Duke's fragile state.

He glared at her, then faced Tom Kensey, the shortstop for the Vikings and the best pitcher they had beside Duke himself. "I didn't make the roster."

"What?" Kensey's cheeks paled, then flushed. He shuddered then slammed his fist into his palm. "I'll fucking kill Baxter. We're nothing without you."

"I'm old, and my fastball's slowing. The shoulder, y'know." Duke grimaced. His last surgery hadn't returned his pitching to what it had been before he'd torn the tendons. Part of him had known his career was on borrowed time, but hope was eternal and often senseless.

Vanilla and the sweet scent of a perspiring woman warned him they weren't alone.

"Drink, boys. I may look capable, but I sure as shit can't carry you if you faint on me." She pulled their water bottles from their backpacks and shoved them into their hands. Skipping a few yards away, she faced the group. "If you're ravenous, there are prepacked bags of trail mix that will tide you over." She raised her gaze to the horizon. "Dinner's at sunset, so not too far away. We'll be camping beside the river and will cross over first thing in the morning. After breakfast, of course." She beamed. "Shall we continue?" With a bounce that jiggled her breasts, she barreled her way up the path.

His ex-teammates huddled as they rehashed last night's party, all trailing Ms. Perky. Duke was the last of their team, ahead of Eli, Finley's father.

The sun had begun to set, and the temperatures cooled with it. The longer they trudged, the louder the river grew until, at last, she called a halt for the day. Around a rock-rimmed fire pit, she helped everyone set up their tents. Her excitement and contagious laughter merged with the cacophony of the evening insects. Too many times Duke smiled without meaning to.

He hurried to build his tent, not wanting to be in proximity to her and her mind-bending perfume. Easy to do when he'd camped with his dads before they retired to South Africa. He paused and arched his back, admiring the eager stars sprinkling the orange and navy blue sky. He would call Dad and Pops with the news…when he had a new phone.

"Need any help?"

His breath caught, trapping her scent in his lungs, and for a moment, he couldn't form a thought. She didn't wait for his response but leapt around him, hammering pegs into the ground and unrolling his sleeping bag. He watched her, admiring the curves of her body as she worked.

"Dinner's one of the prepackaged meals at the bottom of your backpack. If you gather your cook-stove, we'll have you eating in no time." She hesitated. "Sorry, I never caught your name."

"Duke." He could speak. Will miracles never cease?

"Unusual, but who am I to judge." She grinned and left him staring after her. How did she manage to remain so upbeat? Was she on something?

Making his dinner in a cook-stove was easier than he remembered. Once he started the little gas stove, warming up his chicken parmigiana was quick.

"I hope you love the meals. My wife prepares them for each hike." Eli circled the camp, ensuring everyone had managed to warm their food.

Finley emerged from behind a tree, zipping up her camo pants and tucking in her T-shirt. Duke frowned. He hadn't noticed her leaving when the silence should have warned him.

Smiling, he studied his friends as they dug into their dinners, laughing and joking. He would miss this. Putting his food jar and spoon aside, he sprawled out his legs, which pinged at their abuse. He wasn't an unfit man by any stretch of the imagination, but his body thrummed and burned from the afternoon's exertion. It proved that a variety of exercises used different muscles.

"What about bears?" Jackson's voice carried over a lull in the conversation.

"Our bears are part of a research project and have been tagged. We know where they are at all times and plan the hikes to avoid them. After all, this is their land more than it's ours." Finley sat cross-legged on a blanket while she ran her finger along the inside of her food jar and popped it into her mouth for a good suck.

Duke smothered a groan as a heat blazed along his veins to his groin. He crossed his legs, hoping to hide his growing interest.

In the firelight, her skin glowed, and her brown eyes darkened. Her hair turned molten gold. He stared, unable to drag his gaze away. Since she was talking, he had an excuse. Still, he had stronger control than this.

"You have bear spray in your packs for those pesky surprise ambushes." She gathered their food jars and spoons, balancing them in her arms. When she reached Duke, he rose to help her, taking a few from her. His fingers brushed her arm, and energy surged between them, sparking his nerve endings. He stilled, catching his breath and praying she hadn't noticed.

She stared at him with her mouth parted. "You okay?"

"Fine, just received bad news." Why had he mentioned that?

"I'm so sorry." She didn't pry but nudged him with her hip instead of an arm squeeze, or worse, a hug. "I traverse the mountain in search of answers. Often, the solace it provides helps." With the moon to light their way, she headed toward the gurgling river.

He released his breath on a whoosh. That had been close. Stumbling after her, he lowered the dirty jars and utensils beside her on the riverbank. She crouched and dipped a jar into the turbulent water.

"Can I help?"

She flicked a smile at him, bright in the moonlight. "Use the riverbed sand as a scourer, then stack the cleaned jars onto each other."

He kneeled beside her, uncaring that the wet sand saturated his jeans. She didn't speak but let the insects and river fill the comfortable silence between them. His shoulders slumped, with tension easing from his stiff back muscles. The night air was sweet and cool. The moonlight dancing off the pine trees, boulders, tumbling water, and her pale face was captivating.

Peace consumed him, and he smiled, letting the simple action of washing dishes calm his panicked thoughts. So, he could no longer play the game he loved. What did that matter when he had his health and was rich? He could do anything he wanted. Perhaps he was thinking about it from the wrong perspective. This was a forced retirement and not the end of his life.

"I'll head back if you want to linger?"

He raised his gaze to hers shrouded in darkness. "Please."

She nodded, gathered the stacked jars and utensils then strolled back. He watched her until she reached the camp. She could have chatted his head off, yet she hadn't. He was vulnerable, an easy target. She could've made a move on him, but she hadn't. He frowned. She hadn't shown by look or word she was interested in something horizontal with him. What an intriguing woman she was.

Mm, her lack of interest, despite the earlier blush, should delight him as emotionally unstable as he was, but it didn't. Instead, it highlighted how far he'd fallen, that he couldn't even charm a park ranger. The raucous laughter had faded and the firelight had diminished by the time he reached the camp. En route, he took a piss, washed his hands in the river, and crept back to camp, careful not to trip over her precious green weeds.

Greeting him was the slow crackle of a dying fire. Everyone had turned in. Some might be asleep, so he tiptoed through. The first tent he passed was a little distanced from the others, and with its torch on, glowed like a beacon. The scent of vanilla teased him. Just to confirm it was Finley's tent, he peered through the gauzed skylight.

A glimpse, nothing more, but when she pulled off her T-shirt and unclipped a delicately feminine bra... Swallowing a growl, he jerked back, ready to grant her privacy until she cupped her bare breasts on a husky moan. Bolting for his tent, he dove through the opening and spun onto his ass to zip it shut. He shivered with a spark of lust shooting across his skin like a thousand fire ants. Adjusting his cock in his too-tight jeans, he yanked off his boots and socks and crawled into his cold sleeping bag.

Cursed, that's what he was. No job, and now a woman whose bright smile was adorable but her bubbly optimism irritating? No, he wouldn't stand for either. He was man, hear him roar. Smiling, he scoffed at his Tarzan thoughts. *One thing at a time, Tiger.*

And that one thing was Finley.

Chapter Three

Fin kneeled beside the river, this time with Jackson helping her rinse out the jars. Breakfast had been thrown-together bacon-and-cheese omelets with dark-roasted coffee just the way she liked it.

Jackson kept a steady chatter about baseball, of all things. He loved the game, though why he felt he needed to share with her, she couldn't say. Used to men regaling her with the massive accounts they had won, trips abroad, latest creations in the advertising world, she zoned them out. With her first hikes, she had cared what their occupations were, but now it all blurred into too much information she didn't know how to process.

Letting him ramble on as she relived last night with Duke, she smothered a snort. Who named their son Duke? Was Prince or King taken? Regardless of his name, that man was as delicious as gooey marshmallows. She wanted to gobble him up, then spend a few minutes licking her lips.

With a shuddering breath, she forced the heat coiling up from her core to cool. Daydreaming about the man was about it for her. Not that he had shown much interest, but to be fair, she wouldn't know he liked her unless he wore neon signs and danced in the buff.

She grinned, stealing Duke's tats peeking out of his T-shirt and envisioning them on her next male character. Mm, maybe he would be in the mafia but not committed to it. Violent, graphic scenes might cast him as a monster, so those were out, but a little bloodletting would spice it up.

He would meet a woman who wouldn't know who he was or hadn't heard of his reputation. Someone from Africa? She'd always wanted to visit that continent.

If she added extra energy into cleaning the last jar, she could sneak in a few minutes of writing before she'd lead this testosterone-high bunch across the river.

"Thanks, Jackson. That about does it." She gathered the jars and utensils, interrupting him mid-ramble. "So, are you all baseball fanatics?"

"Fin, how can you not know who the Vikings are?" Jackson trailed her, but his shock was easy to discern without meeting his gaze.

She shrugged. "Vikings were big, burly warriors, capable of removing the head from your shoulders with a single swing of their ax."

"What?"

Chuckling, she ignored him gasping behind her as she lowered jars and utensils beside each dismantled tent. Dad had overseen that part of camp since he'd leave her soon. Mom had planned a surprise romantic dinner that she had to postpone. She made Dad's favorite, pulled pork lasagna. But Mom was resilient. Fin had no doubt Dad would be enjoying his lasagna soon enough.

Dismantling her tent, she focused on folding it into its bag. She had rolled her sleeping bag and packed her backpack before breakfast. Anything to buy a few minutes of writing time.

"What happens now?"

At that deep timbre, her heart leapt into her throat, and she squeaked. She dropped the tent and teetered, but two warm hands gripped her hips steadying her. Frozen against him, she nibbled on her bottom lip as she debated raising her gaze to her savior.

Summoning a smile, she twisted and lost her breath in a strangled gasp. Duke stared at her with a smoky intensity in his baby-blue gaze that her body recognized. Heat flooded through her from the tips of her ears to settle between her thighs. Had she been more comfortable around him, she would've laughed away her reaction. She didn't know him, and being this close to him raised the hairs across her body. Where he stood, what he was saying, and where his gaze rested never went amiss. A nervous giggle lodged in her throat. Her vision blurring with dark spots reminded her to breathe lest she faint at his feet. Oh, no, she wasn't one of *those* women.

Images flooded her of Duke in his beige velvet breeches tucked into polished Hessian boots. The wind whipped at his white, linen shirt—unbuttoned and exposing a delicious, tanned chest. Her empire gown was torn, revealing a sinful amount of cleavage. Behind him, a horse snorted, pawing the ground, and in the distance, amid a haze of mist, was his illustrious estate. Mm, perhaps she should give historical romance a try.

"Oh, milord, you frightened me," imaginary Lady Finley crooned, pressing her splayed hand to her chest.

His gaze traveled there before yanking her against his firm chest.

"Unhand me, sirrah." She slapped his arm.

He growled and hoisted her over his shoulder, striding toward his mount with enough swagger to stifle her scream.

"Oh." Fin fanned herself then snapped her gaze to Duke, his chest warming her shoulder. *Holy mackerel.* He'd asked her a question. Racking her brain brought not a single word to mind. She blinked, layering her hands over his fingers gripping her hips.

"Um…" She licked her lips.

His focus shifted to her mouth as if mesmerized.

Lust darkened, whispered, and demanded as it uncoiled in her core. The absurdity that he might find her attractive summoned her sense of humor, and she grinned.

Her sanity returned like the snapping of an elastic waistband, abrupt and painful. "Across the river. Up for it?"

He cleared his throat and lowered his hands, then gazed at the river offering his spectacular profile for her delectation. *Holy mother of pearl.*

"I am if you are." A slow smile crawled across his sensual lips and scattered her thoughts once again.

The man was lethal. Was she staring at him? Had he noticed? A cool breeze brushed across her flaming cheeks, and if she listened carefully, they sizzled.

"We mounted a cable between two gum poles." Dipping her chin to her chest, she hid her fascination while she kept her twitching hands busy. She wanted to run her fingers through his dark chocolate-brown hair. "We modified a canoe so we can pull ourselves across the river with minimal effort." She clipped her tent and sleeping bag to the base of the backpack wishing he'd wander off and leave her be.

Her spine tingled as if he stared at her. "Quit being silly," she huffed.

"About?"

Closing her eyes, she prayed he wasn't standing behind her watching her shove her ass in the air as she finished packing.

She faced him, plastered on a bright smile, and bounced on her toes, trying to appear as excited as normal, when what she wanted to do was stick her head in the sand like an ostrich. "Just having a private conversation. Didn't you mama teach you not to eavesdrop?"

"I didn't have a mama."

"Oh." Pressing her hands to her cheeks, she gaped at him. "I'm so sorry."

He grinned, and she cursed him. Here she was apologizing while he beamed at her like an idiot. Not to mention his knee-weakening smile with his white teeth denting his bottom lip. Shit, there had to be something wrong with her.

"I have two fathers." He captured a curl between two fingers and tucked it behind her ear. The sensation of his touch stroking the shell of her ear froze the air in her lungs. She was sick, drugged, on a high, or a low. "I'm adopted."

She swallowed her tongue under his vigilance. "You must have been an adorable baby."

Pinching her lips shut before she confessed her undying lust for the poor man, she darted around him to herd her clients toward the riverbank. Maybe she should throw him over her shoulder and dart into the forest? She chuckled. Doable. As an ex-nurse, lifting patients had strengthened her core.

"Ready for this?" Dad gathered her into his arms to press a kiss to her temple.

"Dad, not you too." She growled into his shirt, tempted to punch him on the arm if she could reach there.

He chuckled and raised his gaze to the overcast sky. "I mean the river, sweetheart. The weather reports warned of rain farther upstream."

"Oh, it looks its usual turbulent self." She shrugged, which was hard in his tight grip.

Dad was a good hugger, and she loved that about him. He didn't tell her and Alex he loved them but showed it with shoulder pats, ruffled hair, and in her case, kissed temples. Nuzzling her nose across his T-shirt to soothe an itch, she pulled back, asking for release.

"So, up the mountain, skirt the windward side, head southwest toward Old Margot's cabin, then east along Monkfail. Alex will meet you at the crossing."

"Yeah, yeah, the usual, Dad. Why so nervous?" She tugged forward, and they walked arm-in-arm toward the river. "And there will be no stopping at Vincent Falls this time. I want this trip done. I can't wait to snuggle in front of the fire this winter."

"Are you going to see Sam again?" Dad wiggled his eyebrows.

She groaned and pinched the bridge of her nose, wishing she knew how to convince the determined man she wasn't interested. "As much as I love a man in uniform, Sam's fireman outfit doesn't do it for me."

"What? When he's on those silly calendars every year?" Laughter rumbled through Dad's chest until he leaned back to release it. It stampeded through the morning air and summoned an answering smile from her.

"I've known him since kindergarten, Dad, but I can't see us being more than friends."

"He's hoping otherwise. Pestering Patrick to convince you to date him." Dad grabbed the canoe and pulled it toward the water's edge. Dodging the deep furrow it carved in the wet sand, she hurried to help him, anything to avoid acknowledging that pointed look.

Sighing, she dropped the canoe and connected the brackets to the cable. "Well, Patrick hasn't mentioned it." And if he had, she would have nipped that in the bud. "I'll talk to them both. *My* love life. Sometimes I think y'all would be happier if I spread my thighs for every single man in town." It would be a short exercise since she could count on one hand the town's bachelors, and one was her cousin, Patrick.

Dad rolled his eyes. "Just date someone so the townsfolk can busy themselves with planning your wedding and taking bets on what you'll name your firstborn."

Ah, the hazards of small-town life. She laughed and let it fizzle into a cheeky grin. "Yeah, right. I'll just pick one from all the hopefuls lined up. I mean, who wouldn't love a sensual, curvaceous body like mine?" She spun on the muddy sand, swinging her hips, and thrusting out her breasts with a bat of her eyelashes. "Might even suggest we do a Chibougate Tours Christmas Calendar. Alex can wear a sock on his—"

"Silly monkey." Dad shook his head despite the matching grin that split his cheeks. "And don't you dare mention that idea to your brother."

"I can hang Christmas ornaments off my nip—"

"Fin." Dad clutched his chest, raised his face to the sky, and let the tears of laughter fall. "I shouldn't find that funny. Your mother says I encourage your nonsense."

Not worried that their conversation could be heard above the roaring river, nor that anyone was watching anyway, she did a short dance number with jazz hands.

"Mom's worse than you." Still laughing, she faced the men.

They gathered in twos and threes, joking and batting imaginary balls.

Bouncing between them, she gestured to the canoe. "One by one, I'll pull you across the river. Who's brave enough to test the fury of the Mighty Matacona? Superstition has it, that if you cross it in broad daylight, within a day, you will meet your next ex-wife."

Only Jackson chuckled. She sighed. *Tough crowd.*

They blinked at her, except for Duke who'd kept his gaze fixed on her, not once glancing at the canoe. His unwavering focus was mesmerizing. Releasing a slow breath, she kept her smile in place by sheer willpower.

"I'll go first." His deep voice supercharged her heart, spiking electricity to her extremities. Holy corn nuts, she should bottle that and save it for her spank bank. Just removing the bottle's cork might give her an mini-orgasm.

She nodded and darted to the canoe. "Dump your backpack alongside mine and climb in."

He unclipped his pack and lowered it beside hers, then gripped the side of the canoe. With a shove, rippling the muscles in his arms, he pushed it the final stretch into the river. The water rocked the boat more than usual, but she ignored it. The heat uncoiling in the pit of her stomach was due to this man consuming the space in the canoe with his massive bulk. It had nothing to do with the turbulent waves slapping the canoe.

Once they were in, she tugged on the cable and started the crossing, glancing over Dad and the group watching on the bank to Duke still focused on her face. The canoe lurched, and she swung her gaze upriver. Had the water level risen?

He crowded her, arms brushing along hers, to grab the cable, matching her rhythm as he heaved. The canoe cut through the water faster, but dread intensified and thickened inside her that had nothing to do with his masculine cologne. She paused, stalling the crossing two-thirds of the way. Beneath the roar of the river was a growing rumble, and with it, a mounting panic flicked her gaze at Duke, then at her father.

She pointed up the mountain, and above the deafening roar, screamed at Duke to pull harder. He did, no questions asked. The bank was so close. If they reached the other side, they could wait out the flash flood.

Cold water sprayed across her face, and she snuck another glance upriver.

"Duke!" The warning came too late as a dirty-brown tidal wave hit the side of the canoe, drenching them.

The little boat should be fine since the cable and brackets secured it. But they weren't safe. She grabbed the sides when the force of the wave, along with the detritus from a mudslide, tried to flip them into the water. Large, splintered logs slammed against the side, tilting the boat. The backpacks bobbed down the river, bright colors of hopelessness.

Drowned-rat Duke crept across the canoe to her, rocking it further, then looped an arm around her to tug her against him. "We should leap for it, Fin."

She nodded, shivering when another wave broke against the side of the angled canoe. Water pooled at the base, sinking them as well. The cables pulled taut, testing the brackets.

He was right and yet, they hesitated. The water rose, surged, and tossed them into the churning waves. The cold snatched her breath as the currents swept her under. She paddled for the surface, fighting the suffocating panic as objects knocked the air out of her lungs and snatched at her clothing.

Her lungs burned with the need to breathe, and as she broke the surface, she sucked in air. The flow's force carried her down the river at a fast pace, but she couldn't see Duke. Fear, colder than the water, settled in her bones. She screamed his name, wasting her breath since whatever noise she made, the river swallowed before it yanked her under again. Something snagged her shirt, and she struggled against it, kicking at it.

But it held firm.

This was it. This was how she'd die. Drowned near her beloved mountain. She stopped fighting, accepted her fate as her tears merged with the river. Breaking through the surface, she sucked in air, expecting another wave or a branch to hit her, to pull her under. Instead, something dragged her across the flow. A warm arm wrapped across her chest, and she opened her eyes to Duke's pale face inches from hers. She'd never seen anyone more beautiful.

"I've got you, Fin."

Chapter Four

Shivers wracked Duke's body, worsening the shudders of his exhausted muscles. If it wasn't for the hell he put his body through, he couldn't have held onto Fin. The cold, wet sand beneath him couldn't compare to the bone-chilling sense of loss the idea of Fin dying summoned within him.

A similar dread had claimed him every damn day during the summers he spent lifeguarding at the public pool. It had nothing to do with her sensual appeal, the way she'd danced for her father, or thrust out her breasts like Duke needed to notice them more.

His palm was on fire, the only part of him warm. Fin sprawled beside him, pressing his arm into the mud. He curled it around her and trapped her against him. Goosebumps spread across her bare skin, and her teeth chattered through her labored breathing.

"Fin?"

"I...I'm fine." She burrowed into him, searching for warmth. "We...need to move."

He didn't want to. "Just a moment longer. Let me catch my breath." The roaring river flowed past them, like a traffic-laden street, uncaring of the danger it posed to pedestrians.

Splaying her fingers across his chest, she arched to meet his gaze. "Thank you, Duke." Her dark eyes dominated her pale face, and her bottom lip trembled, tempting him to warm it with his tongue.

He raised his burning palm to cup her cheek and froze. A bold red gash from forefinger to wrist seeped blood. He tried to curl his fingers to hide it from her, but she leapt up and gripped his hand while he suffered from the acute loss of her warmth.

"What the cuss." She released him to fumble with a pocket on her camo pants. Her fingers were as blue as her lips. Flicking out a blade, she hacked at the hem of her T-shirt, exposing a ribbed abdomen. He blinked, disbelieving his eyes. Sitting up, he kept his gaze fixed on her frantic movements, hoping for another glimpse that would center his world. A soft, curved belly and silky skin were what he expected. Not an Amazon beneath her garments.

She ripped the fabric and exposed a section of her stomach. Finley wasn't plump at all, despite her wide hips and sensuous curves. Her camo pants molded the muscles of her tree-trunk thighs, and those were abs she had, comparative to an Olympic wrestler.

"I can't disinfect, but if we can reach one of the trails, we have supplies stashed along it." Within minutes, she had bandaged his wound and tucked the end under the strip of cloth.

She flashed her signature smile that had more to do with her mask and her inner strength than her happiness. Something he was learning about her. Clambering onto a nearby boulder, she studied the river and spun on the spot to assess their surroundings, offering an unrestricted view of her ass.

"We're too far down to hike up to the Matacona trail. We should head for Monkfail. The river doesn't look like it'll be passable anytime soon, and we need supplies." She folded her knife and slipped it into her pocket, then jumped off the rock to the riverbank, jiggling her breasts defined by her wet T-shirt.

Heat infused his body, and he shuddered. He twisted, giving her his back as he adjusted his drenched jeans in the hopes the cold denim would hold back his growing erection. "Lead the way."

Instead of turning south, she rested her backside on the boulder and unlaced her boot.

He scowled. "What are you doing?"

"Removing a sock so my dad knows we live." She nudged her chin at his boot. He grumbled and crouched beside her to do the same.

She laughed, patted his shoulder then peeled off her wet sock. "Quit complaining. There are fresh socks in the bear bags."

He stared at her toenails painted in a sexy deep red. Closing his eyes, he parted his lips to draw in silent breaths. Couldn't she have hideous feet?

His hesitation must have come across as pain, for she brushed his fingers aside to unlace and tug off his boot. Her warm touch when she peeled his sock off was more sensual than had she run a fingertip along the collar of his T-shirt.

Her sharp tugs of his shoelaces drew him back to the moment. She draped his sock on the boulder beside hers, both facing the south.

Then she surprised him again by resting her hand on his shoulder. He gritted his teeth. This was ridiculous. She was just a woman with many hidden depths and mysteries, but still, he was the seducer in this scenario.

"Ready, Duke?"

He nodded and pushed himself off the boulder. She stroked his chest while dropping her hand, her touch reaching him through his wet T-shirt. He shivered. With one sock missing, his toes squelched as he trailed her. As if they hadn't dodged dying, she set a steady pace. Instead of watching his steps, her drying clothing fascinated him, more so the bright yellow curls of her hair when they caught the sunlight. The sun beat down, warming him, yet it didn't stop until a fine sheen of sweat coated his skin.

By midday, he needed to rest. They'd clambered over boulders, across mud, slippery pebbles, and grass as they hiked parallel to the river. He opened his mouth to ask for a break, but she paused. After scanning the ground beneath her feet, then the river, she dug out a rock to scrape the letters "M.C." on the footpath.

"This is the Monkfail trail." She laughed, jogging up the winding path. "That tree over there with the red marking has supplies. Thirsty?" Spinning on a heel, she faced him while she walked backward up the trail. "Hurry up, slowcoach."

He grinned and accepted her challenge. With a burst of energy he knew not the source of, he jogged toward her and scooped her off her feet. She squealed and scrambled to grip his hips and waist. He swatted her ass, and her breath caught. For a second, silence prevailed.

"You didn't just...? Duke, put me down!" She slapped him in return.

A dart of need shot from his stinging butt cheek to his groin. He swung her over his shoulder and set her back on her feet. That was stupid of him. He didn't need to know how good she felt in his arms, how much heavier she was, how warm her skin was against his, and how good she smelled with hints of mint and vanilla.

"Why do you smell like mint?" Raising his chin, he sniffed the air around her, searching for the source. He jerked back when he was an inch from her mouth. "Chewing gum?"

"No, wild mint." She hurried around him, brushing her curls across his chin. "Here, the plants with pretty purple flowers." Bending over shoved her ass in the air and exposed her white panties. He stretched out his fingers, hoping to run them along the waistband, but she straightened.

On her palm were a few leaves. Careful not to touch her, he took one and popped it into his mouth. Earthy mint hit his tongue, sharp and potent. He chewed under her vigilant stare.

"The trick is to break off a few leaves and not deplete the plant." She chose one, chewed on it, then shook her hand, allowing a breeze to carry the others away. "Almost there."

He spotted a wild mint plant and paused to break off a few leaves. When he rose, she was gone. Jogging along the path, he rounded a corner to find her untying a black bag from a branch. She was beaming like she'd stumbled on a treasure.

"This is an ursack, designed to be bear-proof. Alex packs water, snacks, socks, and a first aid kit." She sat on the dirt to unravel the knot closing the bag. "Water?"

He accepted the bottle, uncapped it, and took a long swallow. The tepid water was sweet, but he forced himself to stop at half the bottle, not sure if water was available again.

"We've done about two miles along the river, and it's another three to Vincent Falls where we'll spend the night. Tomorrow, after another two miles, we'll reach Old Margot's cabin. It has a radio and is accessible by helicopter."

"Why not take the bag and head to the river?" The thought of another five miles made his bones ache.

"We plan our hikes around the foraging paths of bears. Not to mention other critters I'd rather avoid. This was also the last hike of the season. The nights are quite chilly, made dangerous without fire for warmth. On top of that, I don't know if the river's passable anytime soon."

He grunted. "Fair enough."

She tossed him an energy bar then bounced across the distance between them to tend to his palm. Her touch was gentle despite the sting of antiseptic. With butterfly stitches, she closed his cut then bandaged his hand. He studied her handiwork while she sipped from her water bottle between bites of an energy bar.

"This looks so professional." He gaped as he flipped over his hand.

She shrugged. "Thanks. I used to be a nurse."

"What?" He transferred his gawking to her.

She rose to her feet and dropped a rolled ball of socks onto his lap. "Just going to pee."

A nurse? He stared after her then hurried to pull on the dry socks. Unsure what to do with his orphaned sock, he draped it on the boulder closest to him. How had a nurse ended up as a park ranger? That had to be an interesting story, only fascinating him further. He snorted. Like he needed encouragement.

"Call out if you want to take a 'bathroom' break." She grinned as she slipped onto the path, looped the bag over her shoulder, and offered her hand.

He accepted, and she tugged him to his feet.

The trail dipped toward a trickling stream, which they followed as they climbed up the side of the mountain. She had ceased her constant chatter, confirming his belief that it was part of her mask. Too busy looking for mint, he didn't notice she'd stopped until he slammed into her back. He flung his arm around her waist to steady himself.

She spun in his arms, pressed a forefinger to his lips, and gestured to the two men across the stream. They hadn't noticed Fin or Duke with their focus on their rifles.

Were Duke's lips tingling where she touched them? Yes, but he couldn't do anything about it, especially when her eyes darkened and her cheeks flushed.

She rose on her tiptoes to whisper, her breath warming his chin, "Poachers."

Her body stiffened as if she prepared to strike. She lunged, but since his arm was around her, he caught her and pressed her back against a solid tree trunk. He layered his body over hers, pinned her in place, and clamped his hand over her mouth, silencing her.

"Did you hear that?" A man cocked his rifle.

Duke dared not peek to see if the poachers were coming closer. Instead, he stared into Fin's narrowed and fury filled brown eyes, promising retribution.

"A grizzly don't sneak up on ya, Hank. Quit being a wuss."

Their heavy tread faded, heading toward the Matacona River. Duke removed his hand but didn't release her. He cupped her cheek then caressed her along her jaw to stroke his thumb up and down her throat.

"They were poachers, Duke." She hissed the words even though only the sounds of the forest filled his ears.

"Sorry, Fin. They had rifles, and we don't. We need to contact your father the first chance we get." But he wasn't sorry she was pinned beneath him.

She pinched her lips and met his gaze as she waited for him to shift away. He didn't want to.

Gritting his teeth, he squeezed her waist then tried to unpeel his body from her softness. His breathing became ragged, and instead, he lowered his head to brush his lips over hers. Her breath caught, and her eyes widened. In that second, she reminded him of a skittish colt. He hesitated, wrestled with his control, then succumbed, testing the softness of her lips with his, flicking his tongue along her plump bottom lip like he longed to.

He ran his thumb up her throat, caught and tilted her chin to angle her mouth to meet his. His descent was too slow, but it granted her the time to choose. Her fingers dug into his ribs, and she arched into him. A groan rumbled along his throat. When he pressed his lips to hers, he held his trembling limbs still and let their breaths mingle—hers mint and alluring with his mint and brutal need.

The hot velvet of her tongue stroking his bottom lip catapulted him away from her. With a few yards between them, he struggled to breathe. But he refused to blink, to miss her heaving breasts pebbled beneath her T-shirt, her pink cheeks, and dark eyes. *Holy fuck.*

"If we don't start walking, I *will* kiss you, Finley."

Her lips parted on an 'oh,' and fresh color stained her cheeks. She scooped up the sack and hurried along the path.

He waited, needing a moment to adjust his too-tight jeans. His attraction to her made no sense. He pondered the many reasons why whatever-this-was-between-them wouldn't work. Each one sounded lame like he was making excuses, or perhaps he was running scared. Something about Fin tugged on his heartstrings, and for the life of him, he didn't know why.

Chapter Five

Fin tightened her grip on the sack and tried not to touch her lips. They tingled, burned, and her heartbeat had yet to return to normal. He hadn't kissed her, had he? She shook her head, then dropped her fingers from her lips. Sparks shot across her nerve endings, and shivers raised goosebumps in their rendition of a Mexican wave. *¡Olé!*

Taut nipples and swollen breasts were signs of a woman on heat. But from one kiss was absurd, and the worst was what lay ahead for them. Vincent Falls had a hidden cave behind the waterfall. Safe enough to sleep in without a tent, it was also private. The last time she'd been there, she'd been alone, so one sleeping bag hadn't bothered her.

Sneaking a glance behind her, she lingered on Duke's melted-chocolate brown hair gleaming in the sunlight, his broad shoulders molded into sculpted pecs, abs, and a narrow waist. He had the textbook tortilla-chip shape with long legs. She smothered a breathless giggle. This was silly. An almost-kiss didn't mean anything,

One second, she'd wanted to confront the poachers, and the next, she was beneath a man who ought to be outlawed for his sex appeal and charming smile. Mother of pearl, she had to get her shit together. Considering her urge to kick poacher-ass, maybe kissing her was Duke's way to silence her, to force her to calm. As a tactic, it was an awesome one. No complaints here.

Her body still hummed, and for good reason. Sam's attempt at a kiss had left her bereft as if she was an ironing board he practiced on. She loved him...as a friend, just not... No, seeing him naked wasn't on her to-do list.

Whipping her focus onto the path, she tried not to remember that Duke had saved her twice. She, the park ranger, rescued like a damsel-in-distress? Pinching her brow, she sucked in a deep breath and refused to glance down. If she saw a silk gown, breasts almost popping out, she would check herself into rehab.

The male receptionist, in a too-tight uniform threatening to rip across his massive biceps, would tap his clipboard, tossed his Viking blond hair off his temple, and run his crisp-blue gaze over her body.

"What are you in for?" He ran his pen along the sheet. "Ah, you must be Finley Clarke. Says here, you suffer from hot-man addiction?" He flicked his long fingers at an orderly, just as tall, muscled, with dark hair brushing his shoulders and the shadow of a beard along his square jaw. "Escort Ms. Clarke to Ward '69,' Sebastian."

She snorted. She was *so* doomed.

The sun was setting, and they were almost at Vincent Falls.

As sweat trickled down her spine, the thought of a dip in its sparkling pools lured her more than the need to rest or for a cup of coffee. Chuckling, she mocked her thoughts. More than coffee? Maybe she *had* knocked her head on a rock and dreamed this? After all, someone like Duke never bothered with women like her.

The hiss of the waterfall grew louder when she skirted a moss-covered boulder. Vincent Falls cut into bedrock, pooling at the base before flowing into the Monkfail River. She tied a double overhand on top of a double overhand knot on the black sack to make it critter safe, then looped its cord in a figure eight around the highest branch. Once done, she dipped her fingers into the pool to test the temperature.

Her nipples puckered in protest.

"It's beautiful." Duke paused on the pebbled shore.

"I give you Vincent Falls, our camp for the night." She flourished her arms as if he'd won a car. "Now for the worst part. We need to climb."

"What?" His gaze traversed the fifteen-foot height of the falls.

"Yup, into the water and up behind the falls. Alex nailed in footholds, so it's easy peasy. Want me to go first?" She chewed her bottom lip, trying to smother a smile. Duke looked like a kid who'd just learned Santa wasn't coming this year.

"I just thawed," he grumbled with an exaggerated pout.

She laughed and let the warmth sweep through her. "Galloping gorillas, are you whining?"

"Am not." And ruined his toddler impression with a grin.

"I want coffee. You can follow or stay outside with the stars, snakes, insects, and scrounging bears."

He chuckled. "Those are preferable to horny fans."

She frowned. "Are you a musician or something?"

His jaw dropped to his chin. "Jackson said you'd never heard of us. How's that possible?"

She shrugged and waded into the water, sucking in a sharp breath as ice drenched her pants in seconds. "Quit stalling, Mr. Famous." Diving in to get it over and done with was like slamming into a solid wall of snow. She burst out of the water with a squeal. "Son of a monkey, it's freezing." She faced Duke, circling her hands underwater to keep herself afloat and finding small pockets of warmer water. "Listen, the longer you hesitate, the longer I have to stay in here. Hypothermia isn't made up by Hollywood. It's a legit threat."

"You're like a siren enticing me to my doom." He waded into the water and cursed a steady stream of words she didn't have the guts to say.

She laughed. "Mentioning sirens makes me think you're the lead singer of your Vikings band. But alas, I can never be your seductive siren, sirrah. These vocal cords aren't made for music." She threw back her head and cawed like a drunk seagull.

He ducked under the surface and broke through beside her, flipping his hair out of his face. Sweet dancing dingoes, he had stunning eyes. The longer they stared at each other, the more her heart raced, fluttering a thousand fruit bats in her chest. When his gaze snagged on her lips, she bolted into action.

Swimming across the gurgling surface, she searched for the first metal spike to the left of the waterfall. "Grab a spike and haul your ass up."

He sliced through the water like a professional, sculpted arms mesmerizing as they glistened in the setting sun. Wiping the waterfall's icy spray and mist from her eyes, she latched onto his arm and drew him closer.

"See the footholds?" Narrow spikes climbed the rock behind the waterfall. "If you slip, just fall. The pool is deep enough not to bang your head on the bottom."

"You're confident I'll fail." He smirked and pulled himself out of the water.

She gaped, riveted by the play of his muscles across his back. It took her a try or two before she could do that. Watching him climb afforded her the best view. His jeans clung to an ass Michelangelo could have sculpted. Dipping under the water cooled her heated cheeks. When she surfaced, she was determined to make it up on the first try.

After the day she'd had, the third time was the charm. Her muscles trembled, too weak to impress her companion with her acrobatic talents. Each spike up drew a grunt from her, but the lure of hot coffee and dry clothes drove her until she threw herself into the dark cave.

She hadn't heard him plummet. "Duke?"

"Here." His teeth chattered which should have told her where he was if the muted roar of the waterfall didn't bombard her ears.

"I'll get the light." Rolling onto her knees, she clambered up, hand over hand, and searched for the torch. With one click, light flooded the cave. Duke shivered against a wall. "Fire, clothes, then food."

Carved into the floor of the cave and close to the waterfall was a fire pit with fresh wood stacked against a wall. The light and heat from the fire swept through the cave the moment it burst into life. She blew on it until it engulfed the log, then fed it more, aware Duke had joined her.

"Strip." She leapt to her feet and unhooked a pair of camo pants hanging off a spike nailed into the rock wall. "You get the pants. I get the shirt. It's my brother's hideout, so it only has the items he needs."

With her back to Duke, she yanked her boots off and placed them to the side. Peeling her camo pants off took too much effort and drained her further. Her trembling and numb fingers didn't help when they fumbled with the zipper and button. *Velcro next time.* The sucking noises of fabric releasing her skin filled the cave, but the heat of embarrassment staining her cheeks was welcome, warming her from the inside. Her shirt was easier after that, but she hesitated with her bra.

Leaving it on meant saturating a dry T-shirt, so off it went, landing on top of her sodden clothing. Unhooking the T-shirt, she slipped it on, sighing when the dry fabric thawed her chilled skin. Without taking the necessary time to debate it, she peeled off her boy shorts, then wrung her wet garments out close to the waterfall and hung them on half the spikes provided.

"Are you decent?" Her voice cut through the silence peppered with the crackling fire.

He didn't respond, so she waited, not sure to peek or to give him more time. Struggling not to look, she sifted through her brother's stash of food. Hot cocoa had her groaning, and she put that to the side before choosing two tinned foods. Pots and cups were next, along with sporks—spoons with fork tines. Then something to sit on.

"Decent now?" Unrolling the sleeping bag, she sat on it and used a can to push the T-shirt closed between her thighs. She didn't need to flash the poor man and, leaping lizards, please let him think her burning cheeks were from the fire's heat.

"Yes." His voice was rough.

Is he in pain? Scanning the cave for him, she stilled and let her gaze traverse his bare chest. Celtic tattoos climbed one shoulder and up his neck. The firelight licked across his skin like molten caramel.

"Nice..." She cleared her throat. "Tats. Very Viking." Patting the sleeping bag, she offered him the canned food. "Spaghetti with meatballs or grilled sirloin with hearty vegetables."

"Can we open both?" He slipped the cans from her hands and sat beside her, crossing his legs.

"Of course, and we can swap halfway if you want?" Pulling the tab off the closest can, she emptied its contents into a small pot and shoved it in the fire to warm. He did the same.

Silence descended again, and she arched a brow. "Why so quiet? Cold got your tongue?" It wouldn't surprise her if it had because his nipples were hard. Forcing herself to meet his gaze, she smiled, hoping he hadn't caught her ogling him again.

"Fin, you just stripped in front of me."

Her breath hitched. "Sort of." She lowered her gaze and chose to stir the bubbling food than look at him. "You did the same." She shrugged. "It's that or freeze."

"I get that." He grabbed the pot handles and removed the pots, placing them beside the fire. Then he laced his fingers through hers. "I don't get you, Fin."

His palms were rough, and his touch hot. She frowned. Then why were his nipples hard?

"What's to get?" Forced to meet his gaze, there was nowhere to hide her burning cheeks.

He huffed. "Woman, you're this jumping jellybean looking for all the world like a plump spinster, but beneath your façade, you're a nurse and a competent ranger with the body of an athlete." His focus dipped and lingered on her thighs.

Since he trapped her hands, she had to shift on her ass to cover her legs with her brother's baggy T-shirt.

"Don't—" His voice broke, and he released her to cup her cheeks. "Don't hide from me, Fin."

The air thickened, and she couldn't breathe. Something squeezed her chest, stiffened her shoulders, and coiled heat in her core. What was he doing? What did it matter that he didn't get her? She bit her bottom lip and tried to hold back a tide of emotions she didn't understand.

He tugged on her lips with his thumb, disturbing her nibbling. His body trembled as he released a shuddering breath. She frowned, pressing her palm over his heart. Was he too hot? Was his heart beating too fast? Although, holy mackerel, the texture of his skin was like velvet.

"Are you cold or feverish?" Maybe he'd hit his head in the river? Maybe they had both hit their heads on the same rock?

"Feverish."

She gasped, rising onto her knees. He rolled to his knees too but didn't release her cheeks no matter how she jerked. "Duke, you might be sick. Why won't you let go?"

"Because my fever has to do with you."

She squeaked and halted her struggle for freedom. "What?"

She was free, but only for a second. He slid his hands through her hair to her back, then yanked her against him as he slashed his mouth across hers. Stunned, she did nothing but freeze, disbelieving he was kissing her again.

With a guttural growl she only heard in certain short films of a salacious nature, he dipped his tongue into her mouth. It reminded her of a skittish rabbit like he feared she'd stop him. His gentleness seized her chest and pooled heat between her thighs. The deeper his tongue foraged, the darker and more intense the heat became until moaning, she burrowed against his chest. She met his next sweep with her tongue, parrying him for a chance to absorb his masculine mint flavor, his breath, and the essence that was Duke.

Jerking away, she blinked at him while she sucked in great gulps of air. "Why did you do that?" She pinned four fingers to her tingling lips and barely suppressed a shiver. "I wasn't chatting or saying anything irritating."

A slow smile spread across his face, which summoned an accursed dimple in his cheek. "You think I kiss you to silence you?" He chuckled. "An excellent strategy I should keep in mind."

"Well, don't you?" She huffed and rested her hands on her hips.

Lunging, he slipped his fingers around her throat and crushed his lips against hers. Another groan tore from him. He plunged in this time, no rabbit in sight. She melted without hesitation, succumbing to his forceful tongue and masterful lips.

Him, an Adonis, toyed with plump her, and to what purpose? No, she was stronger than this. She wouldn't let his kisses sway her to 'suffer' through a two-day sex romp.

She broke the kiss. "Kiss me again, and I'll knee you in the groin."

He winced but didn't look away, staring deep into her eyes. "This is serious, Fin." He rubbed his pelvis across hers, and something incredibly hard wedged between her thighs. She stifled a gasp as shards of pleasure lanced through her.

"In two days, you're on your way home, Duke. If you don't stop this nonsense now, the cabin ain't going to be a picnic."

Dang, her breasts ached for him to lavish some of those kisses on them. She folded her arms across her chest, but a whimper slipped past her clenched teeth. They were too sensitive to bear her touch.

"Stop it. I'm not part of the hiking package." She grabbed the closest pot and sat at the far end of the sleeping bag.

"You don't believe I want you." He gaped at her with wide eyes.

"Sure, you want me. A warm, naked woman before you, what's not to want?" She tasted nothing on her spork, and the idea of hot chocolate left her deflated. Crawling into the sleeping bag was the only way to hasten the morning's arrival. Except, she had to share with a man sporting an impressive hard-on. "I don't do one-night-stands."

He dropped onto his ass and took the other pot. "Perhaps you're right. Perhaps I don't think your hair shines around your head like a halo. And no, you don't have the sexiest stomach I've ever seen. Not to mention thighs I wish you'd wrap around my hips. Nor do I want to nibble on your bottom lip like you often do." He sporked a meatball into his mouth and continued speaking as he chewed. "I certainly hate the fragrances of mint and vanilla clinging to your skin. And your chocolate-brown eyes don't summon a fierce need to lose my soul in them." He paused and met her gaze. "So, yes, any warm, naked woman will do."

She'd pissed him off. *Well, good.* No one used Finley Clarke for their baser needs because she was handy, no matter how much his tirade made her heart sing.

For a second, she could almost believe in love again, love for her, that is. Real love versus her stories were galaxies apart. Trying to find it led to disaster, a broken heart, shattered self-esteem, and a career change.

No, she was safer on her mountain and far away from temptation.

Chapter Six

Fuck, Duke could kiss her *and* spank her ass. Lust raced through his body, and he was ready to dive right in, regardless of the consequences. Yet Fin's lack of self-esteem, when he thought her too exquisite, irritated the shit out of him. But what drove him to see spots around his vision was that some ass-hat had hurt her, making Duke's seduction harder than it had to be. Not that he needed sexual release, not after Jackson's party and the bevy of fans Duke had to choose from.

Sighing, he studied her as he chewed on his portion of tasteless sirloin. She was right to remind him their time together was temporary, but at that moment, the future didn't matter. His was up in the air anyway.

Washing up consisted of shoving the pot and spork into the waterfall and holding on tight. She brought a pot of water and put it on the fire to boil.

Her silence unnerved him, and she was wrong to think he kissed her to shut her up. Then again, she could be sulking, preferring to give him the silent treatment than confront the real issue.

"Fine, sex is out...for now." His cock throbbed in protest, but he had to up his game.

She gasped, almost spilling the cocoa powder she spooned into their cups. "Why do I hear a but coming?" Her lips twitched as she smothered a smile.

"I intend to kiss you every damn chance I get." Sharp bolts of fire shot from his groin to his chest. In his thirty-three years, he had never thought of himself as a masochist.

She gaped, and her cheeks bloomed a bright pink. "Why?"

"Do you want to go into it again?" He frowned. "I'm pretty sure I made my feelings for you quite clear."

"Son of a monkey," she mumbled, rising onto her knees to pour boiling water into each cup. Her shoulders slumped when she dropped her chin to her chest. Then with a deep sigh, she raised her gaze to meet his. "Fine, kissing's allowed."

A wave of victorious joy swept through him, and he might have fist-pumped the air had she not offered him his cocoa. As it was, he struggled to hold back a grin.

"But in two days, it's goodbye, Duke." She was too adorable when she tried to put her foot down, but he wasn't deciding anything definite at this time.

"We'll see." Who knew. Whatever this fascination was might have faded by then.

She pinched her lips but said no more, hiding her face in her cup. The cocoa was too sweet, but the heat of it warmed his core, so he sipped it while running his gaze over her.

Eagerness raised the hairs on the back of his neck. Her mouth pressed to the lip of her cup added pulsing heat to his veins. He wanted to kiss her for hours. She rose to rinse the cups then kneeled beside him with a medical kit. He'd forgotten about his palm since it didn't bother him. As before, her touch was gentle, and her movements confident.

"When did you stop being a nurse?" He kept his voice soft, and he was happy he had when she paled. A tremor swept through her.

"I... Not too long ago, maybe a year?" She darted her gaze at everything but him.

"Fin." He hardened his tone, not appreciating being lied to.

"Eleven months and twenty-six days." Air whooshed out as she released her held breath. "And before you ask, I chose to leave."

He doubted that. "Did you now?"

"Holy mackerel, Duke. I don't need to tell you what happened, so you can stop interrogating me." Her outburst startled him, but more alarming were the tears shimmering in her eyes.

"Fin."

She shuddered, rested on her haunches, and wrapped her arms around her waist. "He's a doctor."

Her chuckle was self-mocking and cold. Duke grimaced, not liking the sound of it. Her happier laugh was so much sweeter.

"Charming and popular, when he first showered me with attention, I lapped it up like a stray dog. But his touch turned brutal, leaving bruises no one saw. His biting words still torment me. I was too fat. I wasn't professional enough with the patients. I smiled too much. Nothing I did pleased him." Her sobs echoed off the rock walls as she curled into herself. "I tried harder, believed his promises of devotion were real, that my love for him was all that mattered." She flicked tears off her cheek. "I shouldn't have been surprised I wasn't his only devotee. I quit within the hour of that discovery and ran home to my mountain." With her tears still trickling, she raised her face to the cave's ceiling. "To lick my wounds."

Fury shook Duke's muscles. "He's a fool and an asshole." If that dick had stepped into the cave now, Duke didn't know how he might have reacted.

He lunged across the sleeping bag and tugged her onto his lap. Expecting her to fight him, he tightened his arms and pinned her in place. But she snuggled into him and clung to his chest with her nails scraping his skin. His body responded like the first hit of whiskey, spreading fire from his core outward.

Between insulting the ass, he whispered compliments and sweet nothings as he rubbed her back. Her tears dwindled into sniffles, but when she used the hem of her shirt to dry her cheeks, exposing her incredible thighs, heat engulfed his face. Biting the inside of his cheek, he needed the sting and salty taste of blood to ground him, to bolster his control. Now wasn't the time for his desire to rear its ugly head.

She tugged, and he lowered his arm, letting her scramble off him. When she washed her face by the waterfall, she had never looked more vulnerable. His heart thumped and rippled out a wave of pain. Trying to ease his body's inexplicable reaction, he rubbed his chest.

When she dried her face, she pulled the shirt tight across her backside. With a long sigh, he raised a gaze to the cave ceiling as she had done. What had possessed him to promise no sex? Instinct? Something had felt off, and as he had suspected, a past lover had hurt her. How was he going to conquer this?

Exhaustion melted his muscles and burned his nostrils. He slumped with his eyelids fluttering shut.

"Ready for bed?" Her whispered question opened his eyes.

He nodded and forced himself to his feet, not sure where she wanted him. She unzipped the sleeping bag, and he slid in where she pointed. Pausing for a moment, she stoked the fire before snuggling into him. With her body layering his, thoughts of sleep evaporated. She halfway zipped the bag closed, then pulled his arm around her waist.

Envying her ability to fall asleep in minutes, he stared into the flickering flames with his chin buried in her curls. Every muscle throbbed after the day he'd put his body through. Yet he wouldn't change a thing.

Nuzzling her neck, he pressed a kiss to the underside of her jaw before letting sleep claim him.

Awaking to a woman in his arms was a new thing for Duke. Not wanting anyone to know where he lived, his passionate nights were never at his apartment, and he left the women as soon as he'd done the deed. There was something to holding a sleeping Fin. Her trust was breathtaking.

Light crawled its way into the cave, filtered by the waterfall. The fire had died, taking its warmth with it, but sharing a sleeping bag with her had held back the chill.

She twitched and shifted, rubbing a hip across his morning hard-on. He hissed. Hoping to still her movements, he tightened his hold across her waist and encountered bare skin. Before he could peek to confirm his discovery, she rolled over and pressed her T-shirt-covered breasts to his chest.

Sucking in a sharp breath, he froze, not sure what to do first or whether he should do anything at all. His hand now splayed across her lower back. His fingers encountered smooth skin, implying her T-shirt had ridden up during the night.

She rubbed her nose across his chest while her breath warmed a nipple. He closed his eyes, fighting the lust pounding at his control. The thin fabric of his camo pants was the only thing separating their sex. He wanted to swirl his hips until his hard-on nestled between her thighs. He ached to tear the shirt off her body and taste her nipples, bathing them with his tongue.

She jerked back and raised a sleep-hooded gaze to his face. "Morning."

Fuck. Her voice… He shuddered, tightened his hold, and dipped to sample her lips. She parted them on a sigh, granting him access to sweep his tongue across her plump bottom lip. The taste of her was addictive, and her softness weakened his resolve. Breaking the kiss, he ran his lips along her jawline to her ear.

She moaned and dug her nails into his chest. A growl rumbled up from his churning core, and he tightened his stomach muscles, fighting his twitching hips. He nudged her onto her back, splaying his fingers across her belly. Glancing down, he died a little inside. She was bare. Pale hair dusted her sex.

"Fin." His need was so intense that speaking her name shredded his throat.

"Oh." She tugged on her shirt with heat bursting across her cheeks. "Sorry about that." Before he could stop her, she rolled away from him and leapt to her feet. "Time to pee."

Too fast for him to register, she whipped off the T-shirt exposing her curvy body for a second before diving through the waterfall. A squeal trailed her into the pool. He grimaced, stroking the sleeping bag still warm from her body. How close had he been to seducing her? Just kissing was dangerous, more than he'd realized. He'd overestimated his level of self-control.

Rising, he stripped off the camo pants. Rubbing his hard-on sparked delicious pleasure to sing through his veins. Then with a grunt, he threw himself into the icy spray.

Bursting from the pool, he cursed and yelped, and each lunge across the water to the riverbank drew fresh curses with wave after splash chilling him to the bone. He caught her disappearing pale leg behind a bush and hurried to find a private spot, wincing when stones and twigs bit into his bare feet. A crisp morning breeze rippled shivers through him, but as he stood there, emptying his bladder, the sun kissed his chest with warmth.

He was going to say this was the life, but the thought of heading into the pool canceled his appreciative mood. A soft cry and splash hurried him, and he picked his way to the waterfall. Her head bobbed as she swam to the spikes. Eager to start the last leg of their trip to the cabin, he dived in after her.

Glancing behind the waterfall revitalized his cooled hard-on. He should have waited, lingered, anything but catch her climbing up. Heat coursed through his body as if he wasn't chin-deep in ice water. *Fuck.* The image of her curved ass and exposed sex was forever embedded in his memory.

Following her up, he called himself a fool, a masochist, and a horny teenager. When he stepped into the cave, a towel hit him in the chest. He grabbed for it, relishing the warmth it offered.

"Found those." In her T-shirt again with a towel wrapped around her head, she stoked the fire. "Hot porridge and coffee sound okay?"

"Wonderful." While he dried, she snuck glances with her cheeks glowing. It boosted his faltering confidence, so he slowed his movements, rubbing every inch of his body. By the time he pulled on the camo pants to join her on the sleeping bag, her breathing was ragged. "What can I do?"

"The porridge is the just-add-water kind. The coffee's worse." She grinned, poked the fire once more, then rose to her feet. "Daylight revealed a little more of Alex's cave, and he's been naughty. He has more than this outfit. Regardless, whatever we wear will be wet while we hike to Old Margot's cabin." She dropped a fresh pair of pants and a T-shirt beside him. "It's about a three-hour hike."

He met her downward gaze, and time stilled, dragging on while the crackling fire and his heavy breathing peppered the air. Her brow furrowed in deep thought. She lowered herself and placed a knee on either side of his hips. Startled, he leaned back yet gripped her waist, relishing her weight and ass across his lap.

"Fin?"

Her brown eyes warmed to that of hot cocoa. She cupped his cheeks and traced her fingertips along his jaw, then scraped her nails down his throat. "Shut up, and kiss me, Duke."

His breath caught, but he didn't hesitate to slide his hands up her back. Then he crushed her against him. Spreading his thighs to accommodate his renewed erection, he brought her pelvis closer to his. He groaned and nipped at her lips until she parted them. Swooping in, he plundered her, thrusting his tongue in without wavering. Her demand for a kiss had led to this intimate position. That she'd softened her resolve enough to ask imploded warmth through his chest.

Breaking away, he paused, fighting to breathe. She scraped his scalp with her nails, feathered kisses across his mouth, and dipped her tongue in as if she tasted him.

"Mm, kissing." The side of her mouth curled upward, tempting him to trace it with the tip of his tongue. "I like kissing."

He grinned, rubbed his hands up and down her back but made sure he didn't slip inside her shirt. Her instigating the kiss gave him the courage and patience to wait for her to offer him the feel of her skin. In a way, it was a good thing since this morning's debacle revealed that with one touch, his control shattered.

She gripped his shoulders. "Coffee?"

He nodded and let her push off him. When he did fuck her, it would be his sweetest achievement because she'd ask him to. Yet a part of him screamed caution.

Charming, effervescent, and mysterious Fin could burrow under his carefully constructed shell and break his heart.

Chapter Seven

THERE IS ARCHIVAL FOOTAGE of girls having orgasmic faints when an idol smiled at them. Fin could relate. She was a tight bundle of nerves, the kind that if her phone, set to vibrate, was in her front pocket, and someone texted her, she'd orgasm on the spot.

She snorted. To any observer, she'd look like she was having a spasm attack or doing some sort of dance that was trending. *What a shame. Finley Clarke showed such promise. It's always the quiet ones, y'know.*

Which left her wet, horny, and stuck with a tune wedgy that had no words. And she only knew the refrain.

All right, so there was a stepped-down-from-Mount-Olympus toffee-on-a-stick man behind her she'd give her left ovary to lick like a lollipop. She'd be a fool to give in to the urge. Knowing her luck and the hard-knock school of Bryce, there wasn't chocolate or bubblegum at Duke's center but a lump of coal.

Gripping the bag slung over her shoulder, she climbed over a boulder and shoving her ass in the air. There was no ladylike way to clamber objects, or she'd have discovered it by now. She snuck glances at Duke trailing her. Waking in his arms with her shirt riding up and his lips on hers, just wow. Contentment had nestled deep within her like a full belly and a warm blanket on a chilly night.

And she'd asked for a kiss. Could a vortex to a parallel universe open up and swallow her, please? Holy mackerel, this was dangerous territory—as in guns blazing, arrows flying, and a mother-of-pearl fire-breathing dragon dangerous. What had come over her? His baby blue eyes, or that dark shadow on his jaw, or the way his hooded gaze lingered on her lips with such longing? Sensuality snuck into her mannerisms. There was an extra sway on her hips, and she threw out more seductive and admiring glances like she used to do with Bryce before he first hit her. Could men ooze pheromones? Every whiff of Duke made her want to climb him like a tree, ladylike be damned.

Her breath caught, and she paused on top of the boulder, fighting the wave of fear paralyzing her when she remembered her shattered heart and illusions. Deep controlled inhales and exhales eased the panic gripping her chest like a vise. Slow, steady, in and out until her lungs could expand. Duke wasn't Bryce, but she couldn't say for sure. She wanted to believe Duke was all gooey inside.

"Y'know, we've been together for almost forty-eight hours." He sipped from his bottle of water, his gaze on her. "If we subtract the sleeping hours and assume dates last for about four hours each, we've been on eight."

She forced a chuckle, summoning her bubbly mask to hide behind. "That's what you're thinking about? Not how beautiful the mountain is, or how sweet the air?"

"It was that or how sexy your ass is." He shrugged, but a charming smile split his cheeks.

She accepted his offered bottle for a sip and tried not to focus on the fact that her mouth rested where his lips had been a second ago. "You have a one-track mind." Returning the bottle to him, she dragged her gaze away from his blue eyes and pointed up the ridge. "Another hour or so, and we're there."

"What will you do first?" His grin dazzled her, and she blinked, almost forgetting he'd spoken, like a deer in headlights.

Offering him her hand to help climb the boulder, she bought herself time to gather her thoughts. "While you shower, I'll radio my father, just to let him know we're alive. He'll arrange the evac." She scanned the thickening clouds crossing the sky and the branches of the trees shifting in the wind. "The weather might not be optimal for an airlift."

Flicking a glance at Duke caught him admiring her upturned face. Shyness gripped her, and she trudged ahead. Giving him her back hid her interest. At this rate, she'd need a cold shower to prevent internal combustion. Where was the tarpit when she needed one? Millions of years from now, some poor archeologist would find her mummified corpse with her nipples still hard.

His confirmation that he watched her ass forced her to walk as normally as possible despite her wet camo pants chafing her inner thighs. From the bones of her bra, the underside of her arms were as raw. She needed aloe vera stat. Chuckling, she thought of telling him that was the first thing she'd do when they reached the cabin. Imagining his expression carried her for a few minutes.

The initial burst of attraction where the man was on his best behavior was the safest for her. She didn't know if she could trust her heart yet. Then again, if she didn't take the leap, she'd migrate from meet-cute to meet-cute, never venturing beyond that point. That wasn't a healthy view of her future, and as a romance writer, long-lasting love was what she longed for.

But grabbing it came with risks.

Was she ready to spread her chafed thighs for a gorgeous singer? Did she want more from him? Eight dates he'd said, and in a way, he was right to mention it. She knew as much about him as an eight-date relationship would reveal. She had slept with Bryce on date five. Admittedly, those had happened over a few weeks, not in two days. And lust hadn't driven her to lose her mind. Not like Duke's potent kisses did. Son of a monkey, the man could kiss.

He hadn't mentioned something longer, and she was safer with short-term, right? If she pretended they'd only ever have today, she could succumb to his seduction. Sadness darkened her soul just as the sun disappeared behind the clouds, casting her in shadow. She shivered and increased the pace. Rain was on the way, and she'd prefer to be in the cabin by then.

The looming thunderstorm mimicking her loneliness was for her knowledge alone.

"There it is," she said, releasing a grateful sigh.

The wooden cabin nestled against a cliff face with its door facing southeast. Solar panels layered the roof, a water tank peeked from behind it, and a stream ran under its raised floor. Large windows remained unshielded since privacy was a given as remote as the cabin was.

"How big is it?" Duke threw his arm across her shoulders. His chest rose and fell from the last steep climb.

"You'll see." She jogged ahead and opened the door, stepping into her sanctuary. Everything was as she'd left it. "To the left is the lounge with corner couches and the leather lazy boys. I curl up in them when I'm reading." She whipped around him to close the door. "The kitchen has a gas stove and fridge. The sink has plumbing, drawing from the rainwater tank out back." A door led off the kitchen to the storeroom, holding firewood and other supplies. "The fireplace is in the bedroom." She pointed past the bathroom door to the bedroom nestled in the opposite corner of the kitchen. Floor-to-ceiling windows lined the wall to afford her the best views when she woke up.

"Impressive." He crossed the wooden floor to peer inside the bathroom. "Whoa, nice shower."

"With gas-heated water." She smiled. "Might as well head there now. I'll radio Dad and start on lunch."

When Duke closed the bathroom door, she released her breath in a whoosh. Dropping her bag onto the kitchen table, she hurried to the CB radio to the left of the stove.

"Margot to Base, come in." Depressing the mic, she darted to the fridge and pulled out a soda, then held it to her heated cheeks. "Margot to Base, come in." She popped the can and drank deeply, moaning when the sugary sweetness coated her tongue.

"About time you checked in." Mom's voice crackled. "How are you, honey? Over."

"Duke and I are fine. Any chance of an evac for the man? Over." She dipped her head, cradled the mic closer, and hoped Duke wasn't eavesdropping. With the shower running, she doubted it. Still, she didn't want him to know she was sending him back alone.

"Just the client? Over."

Fin cleared her throat. "I made it to Margot's, so I'm staying for a while. Over."

"Ten-four. I'll get your dad on that evac. Weather's looking dodgy, sweetheart, might only be tomorrow morning. Over."

"No worries, Mom." One more night with Duke, as she had wanted. "Let Dad know we spotted two poaches downriver from Vincent Falls. Over."

"Copy that. A gentleman would like to speak to the client. Over."

"Break." *Shit.* "Duke!" She twisted to study the door, praying he heard her above the shower. When it didn't switch off, she placed the mic on the counter and knocked on the bathroom door. "Someone wants to talk to you."

He switched the shower off, and the door opened as he wrapped a towel around his hips. She blinked, trailing droplets trickling down his body, like a dehydrated panther. An overwhelming, primal urge assailed her, to trace her tongue over molded contours. Steam hit her in the face, chastising her for her lustful thoughts. She leapt aside to let him pass.

"If my mom asks, tell her I'm showering." She slipped into the bathroom and closed the door. Peeling off her dirty clothes, she tossed them in the wash basket. Her thighs and arms stung, and she twisted to assess the damage. A shower and a little aloe vera would speed the healing. She'd ask Duke if he had similar injuries. She chuckled when she imagined how that conversation would play out.

Um, Duke, you wouldn't perhaps have a friction burn on your person? May I see for myself? Every inch of you needs to be checked, or else I've developed an allergic reaction to your sex appeal.

He'd look at her like she had taken leave of her senses. She snorted. The rashes would be on erogenous zones only, of course. Might as well make the search for extra sensitive 'rashes' enjoyable.

As the hot water flowed over her friction burns, she hissed but didn't slow her movements. The tension eased from her, tempting her to linger, but she didn't want to run out of water before she rinsed her hair. Once clean, she flicked the tap off, wrapped the towel around her body, and tied a knot between her breasts. She hadn't placed out clothes for them. Had she forgotten on purpose like on a subconscious level she expected to be sprawled naked like an offering?

When she left the bathroom, Duke sat on the kitchen chair, resting his elbows on his knees. He stared into the distance with wide eyes and wearing a silly smile.

"What's wrong?"

He blinked, then lunged, lifting her off her feet, swinging then crushing her in a hug. "That was Guy Lewis, the coach for the Bulldogs."

"Okay?" She tried not to laugh with her face smashed against a wet pec. He smelled of soap and heated male—so good.

"He wants me to play for his major league team." He laughed and swung her again.

She clung to him because to do otherwise meant her towel would separate from her body. And if she flashed him, would he react like a sex-crazed thirty-year-old virgin and take her right on the hardwood floor? She studied the polished wood with a little too much eagerness.

Mom, would you mind removing the splinters from my ass and thighs? What? No, nothing like that. I got them doing yoga.

She grimaced. She'd have to ask Patrick to desplinter her and hoped he wouldn't need therapy after seeing her naked. "So, you're not a singer for the Vikings?"

"I'm a baseball player, sweet Fin." Duke cupped her cheeks, creating space between them.

She grabbed the knot, struggling to avoid a towel malfunction. It was one thing to dream about being brazen and seducing a sexy client. It was another thing entirely when the moment to do so arrived sooner than anticipated.

His nostrils flared, and his smile faded. His blue eyes darkened, and slowly, he lowered his head, capturing her mouth with his. A groan rumbled up from his belly, and he crushed her in a hug again, trapping her hand between them. He plucked her lips, swept his hot tongue across hers, traversed the recesses of her mouth, and with each flick, dip, delve, her senses unraveled, her muscles tensed, and something so incredibly addictive uncoiled in her core. She clung to him, unable to think. The kiss went on for ages as if he could distort time. Between forages, her breathing came in gasps.

Thunder boomed, breaking the kiss. She pulled out of his embrace, clutching the knot in case her towel combusted. The cabin darkened seconds before rain pelted down. "There are clothes in the bedroom, next to the fireplace. If you can start a fire, that would be helpful."

Ignoring his grasping fingers, she danced away from him to put pasta onto boil. His fading footsteps gave her the time to calm her breathing. One more day. She could do this.

Chapter Eight

RAIN PATTERED ON THE windows and roof, the fire crackled in the background, and with her belly full of warm, comfort food, she curled into the lazy boy. Duke sat opposite her, legs outstretched on the couch, reading the first novel she'd ever published.

"I can't believe you have these." He smiled, flipping to the next page. "My dad, Liam, loves F.C. Margot."

Warmth spread through her, and she beamed. Meeting a fan was a precious thing, to be cherished and stored for her imposter-syndrome moments. "Tell me about your fathers."

"Pops is the handyman, always fixing something. Despite being a top executive, Dad's the nurturer, loves romance novels, decorating, and flower arrangements. When his company offered him a transfer to South Africa, they took it."

"South Africa?" She gasped, snapping her journal shut. With Duke the Adonis sprawled in front of her, she hadn't written a word of her next novel anyway. "I've always wanted to go there. Have you been?"

"Yup, I head to Cape Town at least once a year." His blue gaze rested on her, but since she'd draped a blanket over her lap and wore her sleep shirt, there was nothing for him to see. Yet, his gaze lingered, and she struggled to smother a shiver of anticipation. With a tug on the blanket, she hid her nipples which kept pebbling her shirt in a look-at-me way.

"And this Guy Lewis, aren't you on a team already?" She gathered her hot cocoa off the coffee table and sipped it. "Jackson's Vikings."

He pinched his lips. "I was, but they released me from my contract two days ago."

"Why?" She frowned. He was a fit man, and she didn't doubt that he had talent.

"Too old." He grinned. "Thirty-three, in case you were wondering."

She gasped, and rising fury flushed her cheeks. "What bullspit is this? That's not old at all. Didn't the greats play until they were in their forties?"

He gaped. "I thought you didn't know who we were."

Ice lambasted her neck, and she forced a shrug. "I don't, but my dad watches baseball, and I listen in sometimes." Pursing her lips, she opened her journal, trying to hide her lying. True, she didn't know who the Vikings were, but she had done a little research on baseball. She'd considered writing a sports romance series and had googled retirement ages. In the end, all their jargon had driven her to choose a more comfortable theme.

"It devastated me, of course. I love the game, always have." It showed in the softening of his eyes and the easy smile he wore.

"I'm happy for you, Duke. Sounds like they've noticed your talent."

"Thanks, Fin." He fluffed a cushion and sprawled onto the couch again. "I'm surprised by how much I'm enjoying this novel. Strange that the author's name is also Margot. Any relation to this cabin?"

She laughed, shaking her head. "Margot was my great grandmother, so no, she didn't write these novels."

Having just lied about her research, she wasn't sure about keeping this from him. Did it matter? After all, they weren't a couple. Yet he'd said he was enjoying it. And if he was going to be an ass like Bryce, she'd rather she knew upfront.

Drawing in a deep breath and with her gaze fixed on his, she took the plunge. "I did."

He jerked, sitting up in a smooth motion with his abs rippling under the gaslight. "What? You're F.C. Margot?"

"Finley Clarke Margot." She thumped the journal on her thigh. "I write in these, then Mom types them out."

Duke studied her, with his blue eyes darkening. A slow smile split his cheeks. "Dad's going to lose his mind."

Her shoulders slumped as relief eased the tension from her body. He didn't disbelieve her, and he hadn't judged her either. When Bryce had stumbled on one of her journals, he'd burned it. No woman of his wrote smut. She'd cried for days.

"Base to Margot, come in." Dad's voice sliced through the cabin.

Grateful for the intrusion, she tossed the blanket aside and scrambled for the radio. "Margot to Base, over."

"How's my girl? You two had me worried, then we spotted the socks." Dad chuckled. "Good thinking. Duke's teammates wanted to cross the river and mount a rescue. Over."

"All's good, Dad. Did Mom tell you about the poachers and the evac? Over."

"Sure did. Got Russ on standby. As soon as the weather clears, he'll airlift you." Dad cleared his throat. "Duke's team awaits his return, along with this Lewis guy. Let me know if you need anything, Finny. Over."

"Will do, Dad. Love you. Out." She sighed, tapped the mic on her temple before clipping it into its cradle.

"What's bothering you, jellybean?" Duke's voice to her left froze her, and she faced him, not sure how to explain she didn't want to think about him leaving in the morning.

Thunder rattled the windows, and bright lilac lightning illuminated the pelting rain.

She winced. "Have you had enough to eat?" It was only two in the afternoon, but with the dark clouds, no sunlight penetrated, and it felt later as if dusk was near.

"Fin." He arched a brow.

"Nothing," she lied, keeping her gaze steady. A shifty eye would give her away. "Was wondering if I should nap or write."

"Fin." He scowled. "Don't lie to me."

She huffed. "How can you tell?"

He stroked his thumb across her eyebrow. "This twitches." He rubbed her cheek. "A beautiful pink splashes your cheeks." His breath caught, and he pinched her chin, lifting it. "When I first saw you, I knew you'd be trouble."

She nibbled on her bottom lip, remembering her first sighting of him. Bouncing on her toes, she forced a bright smile and tried to free her chin. His grip tightened, then he brushed his mouth across hers.

"Mm, now you taste like chocolate." With a flick of his tongue, he deepened the kiss, groaning when she splayed her fingers across his chest. "Tomorrow, it's back to civilization?"

She nodded, then squealed when he scooped her into his arms, carrying her to the bedroom. "Duke?"

He lowered her onto the bed before crawling beside her. "Kisses until then, Fin."

She shivered at his hoarse voice, his intense blue eyes, and his fingers squeezing her hip.

"If you want more, you have to ask." He closed his eyes. Pain twisted his features, and his nostrils flared. "I'm not strong enough to be the voice of reason for us both."

His confession tore through her, crumbling the last of her resistance. She cupped a cheek and ran the pad of her thumb across his bottom lip. "I think after eight dates, I can put out."

He stilled. "What did you—?"

"Alex might have left condoms in the nightstand. If he did, then we're good to go." She clambered over Duke to open the drawer. Excitement shot through her at the stack of condoms, the same time Duke slapped her butt cheek. She gasped, flipping over to glare at him.

He caressed his palm from her knee, along her outer thigh to her hip, taking her nightshirt with it. "This is what I want, Fin." He trailed a fingertip over her stomach, tracing the dips of her abs. "You have such a beautiful body, so soft yet defined." He wiggled to follow his finger's path with kisses, setting her skin ablaze. A groan rumbled upward when he nudged her shirt out of the way, his lips seeking the underside of her breast. "I knew if I touched your skin, it would be my downfall." He lunged up to kiss her, capturing her tongue in the process. "I love kissing you."

She smiled. "So I've noticed." Gripping his shoulders, she allowed him to spread her thighs apart with his knees. A hiss escaped when his pants rubbed her chafed skin.

He paused and leaned back. "That looks painful."

She didn't want her wounded skin to deter him. "Just your pants brushing against it."

"Are you asking me to drop my pants, Fin?" He smirked, but his blue eyes darkened. "If I do that, burying myself in you will happen too fast." He pushed off the bed but returned with the aloe vera and a damp cloth.

She shook her head. "I put some on after the shower."

"A little more won't do any harm." With the gentlest of touches, he patted her thighs, forcing her to spread them wide. His hands trembled, but she couldn't focus on that, moaning when the cool cloth soothed the stinging.

"When you're done..." She peeled off her nightshirt and raised her arms, revealing the chafed skin there.

"Shit, jellybean, why didn't you say anything?" He pressed the cloth to the undersides of her arms.

She closed her eyes on a blissful sigh. "What could either of us do, Duke?"

Cool air caressed her skin, and she opened her eyes to watch him blow across her burns. The gesture was sweet and arousing, pulsing shivers, then goosebumps. Her nipples puckered, and he paused, dipping to suck one into his mouth. With each tug, a cord twanged between her sex and the nipple, spiking her need. She writhed and arched, begging him with her body not to stop.

He did, leaning back to squeeze out a dollop of aloe vera onto his forefinger. Kneeling, he shifted, turning his focus on her thighs. As he smeared the ointment, he blew on her exposed sex before nuzzling her there with his chin.

She raised her pelvis, pleading for his touch.

"If I kiss you here, does it count as kissing?" His voice had deepened to a growl.

"Since we have condoms, you can do more than kiss me."

He tossed the cloth and tube of ointment to the floor and slashed his lips across hers while he cupped a breast. Mimicking the flicks of his tongue, he thrummed her nipple with his thumb. His mouth drowned her whimpers, but when he trailed a finger from her breast to her sex, her breath froze. Heat burst from her belly outward in anticipation. If he touched her at the center point of her need, she might explode.

Galloping gorillas, she couldn't remember when last she'd an orgasm.

He rubbed her seam, then broke the kiss to twirl his tongue around a nipple. "You taste...addictive." Her breast smothered his words. "I can't get enough of you, Fin."

At last, he slid his finger between her lips and brushed her nub. A fiery need slammed into her, and her scalp tingled at his continued onslaught. He swirled, rubbed, teased, and pinched until she couldn't breathe anymore. Pleasure circled her vision and strangled her voice. When he dipped a finger into her channel while resting his thumb on her nub *and* sucked on a nipple, she exploded. The sensations were too much, too intense, too exquisite, and she screamed his name, shuddering when he didn't stop.

Something uncoiled in the pit of her stomach, demanding more like a ravenous beast. She ached within her core, needing him to fill the hollowness. Air chilled her body, and she blinked her eyes open. He stripped off his pants and peeled on a condom.

"I'll try to be gentle, sweet Fin." He nestled between her thighs, his skin not irritating her burns, but he lifted each thigh, resting them on his chest. Positioning his cock at her entrance, he lowered the head and groaned, arching his back as his fingers dug into her hips.

He pushed in inch by inch, rubbing his cock along her sensitive nerve endings. She writhed, begging him to hurry. He didn't but continued a cautious entry. The control he used trembled his shoulders, but he bit his bottom lip and persevered.

"You're so tight, hot... So good." He closed his eyes, drawing in deep breaths. "Don't move, jellybean."

Her breath caught, and she obeyed without hesitation. With one final thrust, he buried himself to the hilt. A scream tore from her, and she bucked, arching off the bed. Pleasure engulfed her, drowned her mind, coated her heart, and saturated her body to the depths of her bones. She gasped when he withdrew and moaned when he plunged in, slapping his balls against her.

It was too much, all of it, yet as another orgasm barreled toward her, the chains around her soul loosened. Something sweet, fuzzy formed for the man who cared enough to protect her skin. The intensity culminated in a monstrous wave, and she cried out, riding it into the heavens. Each nerve-ending screamed she wasn't alone, heightened the feel of his heated skin, his movements, his hips stilling, his deafening roar as he plummeted off the cliff and into the sea of divine bliss.

She drifted down, carried on a kaleidoscope of fireworks and sparks. Buried beneath a hot body with his cock still inside her, a tear slipped past her defenses. Her nose twitched, and she bit the inside of her cheek, fighting for control.

Flitting from one meaningless meet-cute to another wouldn't be possible for her, not when she'd given her heart so easily. Panic crushed the breath from her lungs, but she ignored it, throwing her arms around him for a hug, cherishing this moment as her last.

No matter what tomorrow brought, Duke could never find out that she was in love with him.

Chapter Nine

FIN DIDN'T MOVE AND didn't complain when Duke crushed her with his weight. He couldn't bring himself to roll off her. Her curves pressed into his edges like he'd longed for. Her fingernails grazing his back sent shivers over his skin. Through it all, mini-tremors racked his body from his balls to his semi-hard cock. His orgasm had taken everything from him, melting his muscles and leaving behind a puddle of detonating sensations. One of the best orgasms he'd experienced in a while.

The same sense of victory and accomplishment swept through him at a home run and the adoration of the crowds. Yet as tingles gripped him, he instinctively recognized that lying here with Fin was deeper than that and more precious. When he rolled onto his back, he took her with him and sprawled her across his chest. He told himself that he didn't want to smother her, when in fact, he didn't want to break contact.

She snuggled into him, kissed his chest, and sighed.

Her silence alarmed him, and he snuck a glance. With her face in his neck, reaching her temple was all he could manage. There, he brushed his lips across her soft skin. Her hip filled his palm, and a sense of rightness engulfed his soul. He'd expected one and done, but the lassitude settling him deeper into the mattress didn't drown the certainty that he was far from done with Fin. He wanted more of this, more cuddling and fucking.

Hell, if it meant he drove to see her every free time he had, then so be it.

A frown marred the bliss still pulsing through his veins. She hadn't asked for more time with him nor suggested an official date. Instead, she'd stated their relationship was short-term, a fleeting connection before they parted ways.

The sharp pain skewering his chest gritted his teeth.

He wanted her, and he hadn't realized how much until now. When her breathing deepened, a smile burst across his lips, and he drew her closer. Letting her nap, he considered his options. He didn't know how to convince her to take a chance on him when her last relationship had left her scarred. First, he had to force himself into her life, so investing in Chibougate Tours was a given. A hands-on approach was the best if Eli agreed.

Once he explained how he felt about Fin...

He stilled and twisted to admire the curve of her cheek, her parted lips, the curls of her white-gold hair, and her hand resting on his chest. How *did* he feel about Fin? A breathlessness grasped his lungs, like a thousand trapped moths with their panicked wings pummeling his insides. He snorted at his poetic thoughts.

She stirred, drawing him to the moment. The sky had darkened with the thunder continuing its tirade. Her hand fluttered, then she rubbed his pec with a sigh.

"Did I sleep?" Her husky voice caressed his senses.

"Just a little bit." He stroked her jaw to her chin and tilted it to meet his descending lips. A brush of his mouth across hers to inhale a piece of her soul, that's all he'd take for now. "How do you fall asleep so quickly? I envy that."

She chuckled and sat up, splaying a hand across his abs. Her bare shoulder, the curve of her breast, and her puckered nipple snagged his attention. She didn't seem to notice his appraisal as she finger-combed her curls.

"I was a nurse. I learned to sleep anywhere." Scooting across the bed, she scooped up her nightshirt and pulled it on.

Raising her arms above her head lifted her breasts as well, and when she arched, his cock hardened. He lunged for her, but she pushed off the bed, leaving his fingers grasping air.

"What do you feel like for dinner?" She threw a glance over her shoulder and stilled, running a hooded gaze over his naked body. "Wow, Duke, you're beautiful."

Heat blossomed in his chest like a sunflower in full sunlight. "Come here and say that."

Her mouth parted on an 'oh.' She rested her knee on the edge of the bed before crawling toward him. He flipped her, sprawling across her to nip her bottom lip.

"Fin, say I'm beautiful."

A mischievous smile crinkled the laugh lines around her eyes. "I'm beautiful."

"Yes, you are, jellybean." His sincerity must have struck her because her humor faltered. She dipped her gaze as if she didn't believe him. "I don't need to convince you. My opinion of you hasn't changed."

He was lying. His opinion had evolved into something deeper. Was he a fool to hope for more? Or was her lack of knowledge of his fame the incentive?

She knew who he was now, yet that hadn't altered her treatment of him. No gushing, fangirling, or seductions, although, that might have been entertaining. If Fin decided to seduce him, he'd succumb before she undid the first button.

He caressed her hip, then caught her shirt when he ran his fingertips along her waist to cup her breast. She moaned, spreading her thighs to accommodate him. As he slid into the cradle, he stifled a groan. He was hard and ready to go again like he hadn't a few hours ago eased the burn of lust. What was she doing to him?

Sampling her soft lips swollen from his kisses and testing their plumpness with his tongue consumed his focus and every thought. There was something magical about her.

"I would've been content to just kiss you, Fin."

A smile blossomed across her cherubic face, curling her lips and twinkling her eyes. This wasn't her mask, the one she'd worn when they first met. This was the real Finley Clarke. Adorable.

She ran her fingers through his hair, scraping her nails over his scalp. Her fascinated gaze trailed her touch. He closed his eyes, enjoying the innocent caress.

"Fin." Her name tripped off his tongue.

She focused on him, and her brown eyes warmed to the richness of hot cocoa.

"Duke." She grinned. "Such a silly name." Cupping his cheeks, she stroked her lips across his, peppering kisses on his dimpled chin and along his jaw.

He let her, enjoying her attention, basking in the timelessness of it. Cocooned by the thunderstorm, he settled into her warm embrace, cherishing her curves and valleys cushioning his harder edges.

"It's Dante Delaney. Duke's a nickname."

She chuckled. "Dante? Oh, I love that."

Her feathering her fingers over his ears summoned a shiver that shot to his balls. He groaned and snagged her lips for a deep kiss. Breaking away, he pressed kisses to her temple, cheek, and chin. Nipping her where her neck met her shoulder drew a moan from her. She trembled and dug her nails into his upper arms.

When she rubbed his ass with her heel then wrapped her legs around his hips, his cock dipped into her wet and heated sex. He gritted his teeth, fighting the urge to thrust in like his clamoring senses demanded. "Jellybean, I need you." His rough voice threatened to shred his vocal cords.

"I am yours,...Dante."

His name in her sexy voice tore through him. He growled and plunged in, burying himself until he could no more.

She cried out, raised her hips, and tightened her legs around him. "Please, don't stop."

"Fin." Driven by pure desire and the promise of pleasure on the horizon, he withdrew and thrust in.

She mewled and scraped her nails down his back to his lower spine. Her touch ramped his desperation, and goosebumps tingled from his balls to the head of his cock. No, she had to come first. He wasn't an untried schoolboy. Gritting his teeth, he mustered his dwindling control.

With a slow swirl of his hips, he listened to her breathing, waiting for her gasp, a tremor, anything to show he'd found a sensitive spot. Her channel clenched around him, and he growled. Finding what drove her wild didn't help his flailing control. Taking his time, he slipped out, then plunged in again, hitting that same spot. And again, like tossing the ball at the catcher, on target each time.

She whimpered. Her hips rose to meet his thrusts. Strike one.

She arched her back, smashing her breasts against his chest, and sparked his senses. Strike two.

She stilled, her eyes widened then narrowed. His real name dripped from her lips, like a caress, a litany of worship seconds before she splintered, shuddered, and thrashed in his arms. Strike three.

Her release drenched him with heat, rippled along his cock, and rushed the orgasm he'd held back by sheer will. Unguarded, he roared and pinned her to the spot with his hips. He arched into her as tremors and twitches pulsed through him, adding a sheen of sweat to his body. His vision blurred. Stars danced around the edges.

Fuck.

Drifting back to reality on a sea of bliss was somewhere he longed to linger. Yet slumping over Fin was as captivating. Planting kisses on her shoulder, he rose enough to capture her mouth with his.

"I love it when you call me Dante."

She smiled, but her gaze shifted from his. "Hungry?"

He jerked back and pushed off her, a sense of sorrow tamping down his euphoria. She pulled away from him, not physically, but her soul.

"I could eat." As he swung his legs off the bed, his flaccid cock bare of one thing drew his attention. "Shit, Fin. I didn't put on a condom."

She shrugged, clambered off the bed, and straightened her nightshirt. It ended mid-thigh, hiding her sweet ass from him. "I'm on a contraceptive injection."

He stared after her as she skipped to the kitchen. Had there been tears in her eyes? Yanking on a pair of Alex's camo pants, he hurried after her. She put a pot onto boil and bread in the toaster.

"Is soup okay?"

He nodded, wishing he could hold her and ease her furrowed brow with a fingertip. "What's wrong, Fin?"

"Holy mackerel, Dante, why must there be something wrong?"

He arched a brow. "Answering a question with a question is a diversionary tactic."

She bounced around him as she took out bowls and spoons, the butter for the toast points, and all with her bright smile. He glared at her, hating that she needed to hide behind her mask. After the time they'd spent together, he'd thought they were beyond pretense.

"I'm thinking about my next book if you must know."

He doubted that, but when he opened his mouth to challenge her on another lie, the CB radio crackled to life.

"Base to Margot, come in."

Duke glanced out the window and sighed. The thunderstorm had ended, making radio communication clearer. Eli must have waited for this moment.

She lunged for the mic. "Margot here. Over."

Eli's voice softened with relief. "Confirming evac for 0600 tomorrow, Finny. Over."

She rested her temple on the counter when she spoke into the mic, as if she was exhausted. "Thanks, Dad. Any chance of a restock? Over."

Eli chuckled. "Already organized, my girl. Love you. Out."

Duke frowned. "Why do you need a restock if we're leaving?"

"Makes sense not to waste a helicopter flight." She clipped the mic in the cradle and stirred the soup before flashing him a smile. As much as he loved her smiles, fake or otherwise, her eyebrow twitched. What was she lying about now? "Make yourself useful and butter the toast."

"Yes, ma'am." He accepted the butter knife she held out. "And perhaps you can tell me why you feel the need to lie?"

She shook her head, sadness darkening her brown eyes. "Not going to happen, Dante. And please, stop pestering me to reveal my thoughts or emotions. I'll share when I'm damn well good and ready."

Silence filled the cabin, and he pinched his lips, hating the stubborn tilt to her chin.

Perhaps he was being a bit overbearing.

He sighed and buttered the toast, choosing to give her a little leeway just this once.

Chapter Ten

AFTER A QUIET DINNER, Fin suggested a game of chess, anything to end the brooding silence. Every one of her questions was met with monosyllabic responses. Dante rose to the challenge. Between each chess move, he kissed and cuddled her, and at one point, thrummed an orgasm from her.

Did she protest? Hell, no, her mama didn't raise her stupid. And not with the knowledge that she loved him and that their time together dwindled. Then again, who was she to say 'no thanks' to a glorious orgasm? Fifty years from now, she'd be a doddering old woman recalling her last orgasm like a trip through Shangri-la. Her poor nieces and nephews... "Aunt, please, not that story again."

Three chess matches later, she lay in his arms as he slept, relishing the sense of security his presence summoned within her.

The night echoed with sounds she usually drew comfort from, but knowing she'd never see him again added a sense of sorrow to the crickets, owls, and the trickling stream beneath her cabin. Loneliness saturated her to the marrow of her bones, and she snuggled deeper into his embrace. The heat of his chest, the weight of his arm around her, and the spicy masculine natural fragrance of his skin represented what she yearned for.

A tear slipped past her defenses, but she didn't wipe it away, not wanting to disturb his sleep. And Dad wondered what was wrong with Sam? She swallowed a giggle that was borderline hysterical. Poor Sam, she hadn't been fair to him, hadn't given him a chance.

Perhaps she could in a year or two when she healed from Dante stealing her heart. Twisting, she studied his face in the silver moonlight and the golden glow from the fireplace. She'd made the right decision to stay behind, to avoid the awkwardness of reality returning. Visions tormented her.

In a disheveled Victorian gown in a shocking buttercup yellow, she collapsed at his feet, clinging to his velvet-encased thigh, her chignon unraveling, her cheeks rosy, begging him to stay.

"Milord, I beseech you. Do not forsake me in my time of need."

She sighed. Writing historical romance was in her future if the past few days were anything to go by.

But he was a good man, not a philandering wastrel out to steal her virginity. He would try to let her down gently. She couldn't see him breaking hearts to mark his bedpost. He knew what he wanted and went after it. Her lying naked beside him was a case in point. No sex, just kisses. She'd fallen for that approach, and thinking about the number of times he may have used it on other women led to a deeper sadness she couldn't thwart.

No, this was for the best. He was a baseball player, and women did flock to fame or surgeons. She couldn't judge him on his past interactions, though, when she was inclined to tar him with Bryce's brush. It wasn't fair on Dante, but as a single woman with a scarred heart, she was cautious to venture out of her comfort zone. Then again, would he have noticed her had they not been stranded together? She could've danced the hula, naked, with fairy lights in her hair, and he wouldn't have twitched an eyebrow. And she didn't put an ounce of faith in his supposed interest in her. Her hair glowed like a halo? Pfft, he sure knew how to wax lyrical. Was there a school for that? You, you, and you, off to playboy classes. The rest of you poor sods will never find a woman's G-spot.

Her thoughts smacked of bitterness, resentment, and yet, deep inside, she wished it could be otherwise. That she wasn't scared to try, that Dante's interest was real.

The sun rose, and she had yet to sleep. Any minute now, Dad would radio her, giving her an hour's warning. She slid from under Dante's embrace and glided across the bed in the hopes of escaping without waking him.

Her tears merged with the shower's hot spray, all in silence, lest he heard her.

His hands on her waist drew a yelp from her, and she spun to glare at him.

"Sorry." His grin was sheepish. "You in the shower was something I couldn't resist seeing. Promise me we'll return to Vincent Falls so I can fulfill my fantasies."

Her chest cinched as agony skewered her heart. There he went with his sweet words, ringing of sincerity. He must've gone to the top playboy school in the country. She forced a bright smile to cover her sorrow. He lathered soap on his hands and kneaded her shoulders, massaging the muscles between her shoulder blades. A moan tore from her, and she arched, offering him better access to her back. He glided his fingers down either side of her spine, cupping and squeezing her butt cheeks before slipping his hands around her to coat her breasts with a thick lather of soap.

He pinched and tugged on her nipples while he nipped her ear, then tilted her head for a deep kiss. A groan rumbled from his belly against her elbow. He spun and lifted her, pinning her against the tiles. The cold porcelain bit into her back, and she arched away from it, thrusting her breasts into the stream of water.

"Fuck, you're incredibly sexy, jellybean." He latched onto a freshly rinsed nipple, sucked it deep into his mouth, and ripped a cry from her as a bolt of need shot from her breast to her sex.

With a shove to his chest, she lowered her legs and twisted to grab the soap. The chance to touch every inch shouldn't be missed. She lathered her hands and ran them over every contour of his chest to his sculpted torso. Nor did she miss touching his Adonis belt, trailing his path to paradise before she wiggled free to soap his hard cock, pumping it while she washed his balls. On a guttural growl, he raised his arms above his head, pressing his palms to the tiles.

Kneeling between his legs, she soaped his thighs, dragged her knuckles to his balls before cupping them while she rubbed his perineum. He moaned, his arms and knees trembling. Water poured down his chest, rinsing him. Emboldened by his reaction to her touch, she dipped her head to run her tongue from balls to tip.

"Fin." He roared her name. "You're playing with fire."

She laughed. "What are you going to do about it, Dante Duke Delaney?" Before he could respond, she sucked him into her mouth and flicked her tongue across the head. She gripped his knees to feel his reactions, glancing upward to catch him curling his palms into fists a second before he thumped the tile.

"Killing me, sweetheart."

"Fine, you win." She bolted upright and took a step toward the towel rack.

He gripped her hips and swung her. She laughed, uncaring that his cock, along with his hips, pinned her to the tiles again.

"That's dirty fighting." Crushing his mouth to hers, he plundered her, teasing her with flicks of his tongue as she'd done to him seconds ago.

"Dante, we don't have time for this. Dad's going to radio me soon."

"We'll radio him back." He gyrated his hips, rubbing his cock at her entrance. She cried out, raised her legs to hook his hips, and tugged him closer. "Jellybean, I can't get enough of you. Please...save me."

She jolted, surprised at his words. "What do you need?"

"You, more of you, all the time."

With a quick smile, she cupped his face for a sweet kiss. "You have me pinned to the wall, Dante. How much more do you want?"

He growled, switched off the shower, and carried her to the bed, dumping her on it. She laughed, rising on her elbows to watch him. He clambered over her and spread her thighs wide to nestle between them. His cock pressed at her entrance, and she writhed, trying to impale herself on him.

"Feel that, Fin. Feel how much touching me isn't enough." He slid into her a little and withdrew.

She whimpered, clawing his chest for more.

On the verge of begging, Dad's crackled voice filled the cabin.

She stilled, gazing into Dante's hooded blue eyes. "Fuck me now, or get off."

He laughed. "You never have to ask me twice, jellybean." He plunged in, and she cried out, fisting the sheet beneath her.

Pleasure set her insides on fire, and she arched, smashing her breasts against his chest. A gasp escaped, but she wasn't going to lie there and take it. She wrapped her legs around his hips, pulling him closer so she could drag her nails down his back to his lower spine. She discovered the dimples above his ass, and fascinated, she stroked the dents and rises.

He moaned, his face contorting with a desperation that echoed in her soul. As he pistoned in and out, he snagged her lips for a knee-quaking kiss. Her senses exploded, ramping higher and higher until she wanted to beg him to stop, to never stop. Her hearing dulled except for his moans and grunts, her skin recognized his slightest touch, and every nerve in her channel cried out to him.

She screamed, her orgasm taking her by surprise with the force of it dominating her thoughts. Time stilled, and she drowned in his eyes, in the expression darkening their blue depths. Something inside her snapped, and she lowered her gaze, hiding the love and grief warring for dominance.

"Fin," he whispered, his body tense until his eyelids fluttered shut on a strangled moan.

Something akin to pain twisted his handsome features, and he dimpled his bottom lip with his white teeth. She had never seen anything sexier.

He fell to her side but curled his arms around her, keeping her near. "I wanted to do this last night, but twice a day is my limit." He grinned. "With you."

She puffed out her chest in fake bravado, trying to hide the tears stinging her eyes. "Well, shucks, Duke, little old me, driving you to fuck twice in a day?" She forced a giggle, stroking his chest in a flirty gesture. "I've done gone and broke my record."

"Why, you minx." He laughed and swatted her backside.

"Base to Margot, come in."

She rolled off the bed and tumbled to the floor with an oomph. Uncaring that she was naked, she bolted to the radio. "Margot here. Sorry, Dad, I was in the shower. Over."

Dante gripped her hip and turned her. She arched a brow, but he ignored her, kneeled, and sucked a nipple into his mouth. With a strangled gasp, she gripped the counter as her knees weakened.

"We're on our way, should be there earlier than planned. Over."

Shit, her time with Dante was up. He slipped his fingers between her lips, rubbing her aching nub like he hadn't just blessed her with an orgasm.

She cleared her throat even as she thrust her hips into his touch. "We'll be ready. Out."

The second she clipped the mic into its cradle, Dante snagged her hand and tugged her to the leather lazy boy. He sat and tapped his lap.

She hesitated, not sure what he was asking.

"One knee here, and the other here." He patted his thighs. "I want access to you, I want you fucking my fingers, Fin."

She pinched her lips and tossed a last glance at the daylight spilling through the windows. *To hell with it. One last hoorah.* Climbing onto him, she spread her thighs as she straddled him. He didn't wait, swirling his thumb around her nub as he teased her nipple with his tongue.

Arching as an all-encompassing wave of pleasure swept through her, she cried out, swirling her hips to 'help' him bring her to orgasm.

"Just like that, jellybean." He peppered wet kisses between her breasts. "Don't stop."

He switched between two fingers then his thumb, back and forth, stroking, circling, pinching, and rubbing until she couldn't take the teasing anymore. She brushed his hand aside and circled her nub with her index finger. He released a ragged breath, leaned back to watch her with hooded and intense blue eyes, but replaced his mouth on her nipples with his fingers.

"Come for me, Fin."

That elusive pinnacle he helped build with his tormenting touch and tongue, barreled toward her with her more precise fingers. She groaned as she came apart, arching and thrashing with each wave, more potent than the one prior. Tingles traveled along her skin like a shockwave, trailed by goosebumps with her nipples puckering.

"So damn sexy," he rasped when she settled, her breathing labored. Running his hands up her back, she shivered and let him tug her into his arms. He kissed her, his touch gentle, his tongue slow and thorough.

When he broke the kiss, she pulled away, sliding off his lap with a lingering glance. She wanted to remember him sitting in her favorite chair in the buff. Remember that intensity in his eyes and how her aching heart reacted to it.

"We will hear the heli coming." She laced her fingers through his and tugged him to the bedroom. "Help yourself to Alex's things."

Watching Dante dress was something worthy of an art exhibit, and she lingered for as long as possible until he dropped his ass on the edge of the bed to put on his socks and boots.

She pulled on leggings and a baggy sweatshirt and chose not to strap on a bra since she was staying. Boots without socks followed before she hurried to the door, the thump-thump of the heli blades nearing.

"We'll bring in crates and stack them in the storeroom, ready for unpacking." Raising her face to the sky, she faced south, expecting Russ to take his usual path. "Once that's done, they'll lower a winch I'll buckle you to, then up and away you go." She flashed a bright smile, rocking on the toes of her boots as if energy pulsed through her. It didn't, and despite the euphoria still streaming along her bloodstream, this was goodbye.

Soon, he'd realize that too. The moment she dreaded.

"It's an old Sikorsky HH-52 Seaguard. Russ used to fly for the coastguard, but when he lost a teammate, he retired and now works at the local airbase." The bright white and red helicopter thumped closer and hovered south of the cabin where Dad and Alex had made a clearing of sorts. The side door slid open, and her dad waved before tipping bundled cargo over the side. It lowered on the winch while Russ kept the helicopter steady.

"We're up." She flashed Dante another smile, focusing on his chin.

Scrambling along the footpath, she unstrapped the cargo and carried a crate inside, stacking it in the storeroom. Dante followed her, and five minutes later, she helped him climb into the fall arrester. After clipping him to the lifeline, she slipped the foot loop over his boot. She trailed her nails up his forearm and along his chest, 'checking' he was secure.

With a thumbs up to Dad, the winch took her heart away. Pasting on a brightest smile she could summon, she waved at Russ the second Dante disappeared into the heli's cabin. On the pseudo-casual stroll to her cabin, she let the tears fall without her body language showing she suffered.

The second she closed the door of her cabin, her strength and her knees gave out. With a deafening wail, she crumbled to the floor and sobbed.

Chapter Eleven

WHEN ELI CLOSED THE door on the helicopter's cabin, after unbuckling Dante from the lifeline, Dante knew why Fin had been so bubbly this morning. She'd said their time together was short-term. Their lovemaking had changed nothing.

His vision spun as he fought the rising tide of fury, helplessness, and betrayal slapping across his wounded ego and heart. He'd hoped she'd take a chance. Had hoped their connection had intensified to such a degree that she could envision a future for them.

Not.

He stared with unseeing eyes as Eli clipped him into the seat before slipping headphones on him.

"Welcome back, Duke. How ya feeling?"

Dante nodded, flicking the man a glance. Fin's eyes stared at him. Sorrow gripped him, worse than when he'd lost the opportunity to play baseball. No, that was bullshit. Nothing trumped baseball, ever. His hopes at convincing Fin they could make this work disintegrated like ashes in a stiff breeze. She hadn't wanted more of him and hadn't promised more of her. He was the foolish one to think his kisses had swayed her.

Hell, she hadn't even let him say farewell.

He rubbed his chest where a dark, aching sadness settled.

"The clubhouse is packed. All your teammates, the media, and Guy Lewis are waiting to speak to you. Want to freshen up before seeing them?" Eli's voice in Dante's ears pierced his swirling thoughts.

"Yes, please." He forced a smile. "Thank you for fetching me."

Eli waved a dismissive hand. "No problem. Sorry about all this."

"Beyond your control, Eli. Fin…" Fire cinched his chest, but he persevered. "…made the best of it."

"She's our best ranger." Eli peeked at Russ before continuing, "Don't tell Alex I said so."

Dante chuckled, wishing he could tell Fin that. His smile faded, and he sighed. He had to snap out of it. As good as the sex was, and it was mind-blowing, he had a life to live, one he'd worked so hard for. "Thanks for the evac, Russ."

The man nodded, giving him a thumbs up. "Happy to oblige. Next week would've been a no-go, though. I'll be on my honeymoon." Bright teeth flashed in his swarthy face.

"Yup, Russ is my nephew. I'm kind of looking forward to a little entertainment." Eli wiggled his eyebrows, though, what he was implying was lost on Dante.

"I plan to film it." Russ grinned again. "Fin can't handle her liquor. One sip of champagne, and the dance floor's hers."

Ice pricked Dante's scalp, and he struggled to swallow. He would've loved to see her dance, loved to learn what personality came to the fore when she was drunk.

"You're welcome to come, Duke. If you like." Russ guided the joystick with a gentle touch, and the helicopter dipped.

The forest was a sea of green tips, then nothing as the Chibougate Tours' base came into sight. Many cars, media vans, and a gleaming silver hummer sat in the parking lot where Dante had smashed his phone. Circling the clearing were pathways disappearing into the trees, leading to the cabin roofs peeking out.

His adventure was ending, and he didn't know how he felt about it. He pasted on a smile. "Thanks, Russ. Send me the details. Fin losing herself to music is something I'd pay to see." Maybe then he could confront her and ask her what the fuck was she thinking?

"We have quite a spread, so we'll be landing closer to your cabin. I chose the farthest from the parking lot and the clubhouse for a little privacy." Eli gripped the handrail as Russ touched down. He unbuckled Dante from the seat, then slid the cabin door open.

"I mean it, Russ, send me the deets." Dante slipped off his headphones and hung them on the hook before climbing out of the helicopter. Ducking his head, he ran to where Eli waited. As Russ took off, his blades churned up dust and wind, stinging Dante's cheeks.

Eli led him along a pebbled path to a cabin as large as Margot's. He opened the door and gave a casual salute. "See you at the clubhouse."

Dante frowned. How was he supposed to know where that was?

"Duke." Jackson yanked him into a bear hug, tugged him into the cabin then slammed the door. "What the fuck, dude? One minute you were in the boat with the blonde, the next gone. I almost shat myself."

Dante chuckled, glad to see Jackson. "Yeah, pity I missed that."

The cabin had high-end finishes. A Persian rug warmed the pale wood. Gilded mirrors and plush leather furniture added to the four-star feel. Still, a part of him preferred Margot's.

"Well, how was it?" Jackson nudged him with an elbow as if to say spill.

Dante wasn't ready to talk about Fin and their two days together. "Enlightening."

Jackson threw out his palms. "Whoa, a one-word answer. That bad?"

Dante flipped open his luggage and pulled out a pair of jeans and a T-shirt. He should shower again, but he couldn't bring himself to wash away the scent of vanilla still clinging to his skin. Doing so would be like surrendering when he didn't feel like that at all. He wanted to ask Russ to fly him to Margot's cabin, so he could confront Fin and demand she see him again. On a date, dammit. A legit, romantic dinner, and maybe a movie.

He peeled off Alex's T-shirt and tossed it onto the bed.

"Okay, maybe you meant a good time." Jackson grinned. "You old dog, you."

Dante closed his eyes, drawing in long calming breaths before he twisted to look at his back in the wall mirror. Scratches marred his right shoulder. Fin had marked him. He grinned, allowing the surprise to bubble joy through his misery like air escaping a tarpit.

"Branches from the river, Jackson. A rock scratched my palm too." He flashed his healing hand.

"Shit, sorry for jumping to conclusions. Eli said she's single. Do you think—?"

"No." Dante pulled on his shirt, hoping to hide his grimace. "She's emotionally unavailable. Was dating a doctor, I think."

"Are you sure?" Jackson flopped onto the bed, hanging his boots off the edge. "Some fireman came by, asking for her."

"A fireman?" Fin hadn't mentioned him, so not close to her heart then. "How did he look?"

"Tall, broad-shouldered, with blond hair and stunning gray eyes."

Dante chuckled. "I meant, what expression was he wearing?"

"Oh." Jackson had the grace to blush. "Hopefulness." He nodded. "Well, that explains that." He folded his arms behind his head, ruining Dante's pristine pillow. "Will you ever see Fin again?"

"What's with the Fin-questions?" He frowned, unlacing his boots to tug them off.

"I dunno, man, you feel...different."

Dante smiled, shaking his head at Jackson. "I almost died, so did Fin." He peeled off the camo pants to hide his reaction to Fin in danger, even if it was past tense, and he had saved her.

What if she was in danger again, or those poachers found Margot's cabin? She didn't lock the door, and they could do anything to her with no one around to hear her screams. He gritted his teeth, fighting the urge to sprint for the forest. How would he traverse the river, and could he find the Monkfail trail without help?

He was being an idiot. Talking to Eli about his concerns was the best he could do for now. He tugged on his jeans and sighed, relishing the clean denim against his skin. After donning socks, then boots, he reached for the door.

"No way, fix your hair first. It looks like you were at a brothel."

Dante faced the mirror and groaned. Sex with one woman doesn't a brothel make, but yes, Jackson wasn't wrong to assume a lover had mussed his hair. Not that Dante could recall who seduced who.

"The helicopter ride over." He disappeared into the en suite to wet his hair, running his fingers through his curls until they looked...acceptable. "Happy now?"

He didn't wait for Jackson's response. Instead, he bolted out of the cabin and chose a path leading to the parking lot. Jackson matched his long stride and directed him to the clubhouse. Boisterous laughter filled the air as they crossed the beautiful paving and entered through the double doors. Silence consumed the room for a second, then burst into activity. The paparazzi's cameras flashed, and his Viking teammates shook his hand or hugged him. Shit, he hadn't realized how fond they were of him. Except with Michaels, it was just for show.

Guy Lewis parted the crowd and shoved a beer into Dante's hand. It wasn't seven in the morning. Eli squeezed past, took the beer, and slipped a coffee in its place. He winked as he headed to the bar in the back. Dante grinned, liking Fin's dad the more time he spent with him.

"Your folks are going berserk." Kensey threw an arm across his shoulders. "I organized a new phone for you and left it in your cabin's wardrobe. Welcome back, Duke."

"Hell, no, none of that. Duke's a Bulldog now." Guy squeezed between Kensey and Dante, posing for the press. "I'm having a party to celebrate and need you to sign the contract. I want to lock you in as soon as possible."

"Sure, Guy." Dante grinned at the short man with graying temples and an expensive-yacht tan. The press trailed him as much as they plagued the players.

"Excellent, my boy. We head out as soon as you're ready." Guy raised his whiskey tumbler above his head, and with his wide girth, parted the crowd.

"Landed with your ass in the butter." Kensey shook his head. "You're one lucky son of a bitch."

Dante didn't feel lucky. He'd thought he was when Guy had spoken to him via the radio. But then, Fin had been in the cabin with him. Now, with a coffee in hand, his Viking team nearby, and a bright future looming, it left him disjointed.

Instead of victory filling the void in his soul, it caved like a sinkhole, with its edges expanding.

Fuck, he needed to talk to Dad and Pops.

But to do that, he had to give a speech. Knowing the protocol, he raised his hand, and the bar quietened. Reporters shuffled closer to shove their phones in his face.

"Thank you for such a wonderful welcome. As you can see, I'm well and hearty and about to embark on a Bulldogs adventure."

"Did Vikings release you from your contract due to your age?"

"Was it your shoulder injury lowering your pitching stats?"

"Rumor has it a blonde saved you from the flash flood?"

"When are you signing the Bulldogs contract?"

Dante waved his hand and pointed to each reporter as he answered their questions. "Yes. No. Yes. Soon." Since he had their stunned silence, he hurried to excuse himself. "As much as I appreciate you all caring about my wellbeing, I'm exhausted and wish to phone my dads. They, no doubt, need to hear for themselves that I'm alive."

He nodded at Guy, saluted Eli, and spun on his heel, making a quick getaway. Jackson and Kensey blocked the doorway, aiding Dante's escape. He would thank them later.

He hurried to the side of the clubhouse and tapped on the window by the bar. Eli opened it with an arched brow. "What do you need, Duke?"

"Is it safe?" He dipped his gaze to cage his protective instincts. "At Margot's cabin. Fin's all alone, and the poachers were downriv—"

"Sheriff arrested the poachers yesterday. Alex installed more security sensors and cameras at our weakest entry points." Eli grinned. "Besides, the cabin has a shotgun. She's fine."

"A shotgun?" Dante's cheeks flamed. He was an idiot. No way would Eli leave his daughter unprotected.

"It's sweet of you to worry, Duke." A woman peered around Eli. She was an older version of Fin, except for her hazel eyes.

"Thank you for setting my mind at ease, Eli, Mrs. Clarke." He hurried off, keeping his chin to his chest. Fin was fine. There would be no worried father hurrying to rescue her.

While he meandered the path to his cabin, the silence of the surrounding forest and the lack of footsteps trailing him soothed his agitation. His new phone sat on the wardrobe's shelf, fully charged. No one knew it, but Kensey was a tech genius. He had uploaded all Dante's contacts, so he wouldn't need to try and recall his folks' South African number.

"Dante," Dad answered on the first ring.

With a slow smile, Dante slumped and sprawled on his bed. Peace engulfed him, and he wished he was home with them. "Hi, Dad."

"Hugo, get here. It's Dante."

Pops drawled something in the background before speaking into the phone. "How's my son doing? You okay?"

"When the news said a flash flood swept you away, I almost had Pops book us on the first flight out." As brilliant as Dad was, he was nothing without someone to do the admin part of his life. His head was in the clouds, dreaming of inventions, processes, anything that came to mind.

"Then *I* reached out to Elijah Clarke, and he kept us in the loop." Pops puffed out his chest like a proud potty-trained toddler.

Dante chuckled. "I'm all good. Hiked the mountain, which I signed up for. It was just a more personal tour." Visions of Fin in all her glorious nudity sprang to mind. A *very* personal tour. Fuck, he still wanted her.

Silence met his words, and he waited for them to reveal their thoughts.

"What happened?" Pops asked. "He doesn't sound himself, Liam."

Taking a deep breath, Dante started with strike one. "Vikings dropped my contract."

"No," Dad gasped. "What the hell? Can we sue them?"

Pops sighed. "Relax, let's hear the boy out before you go all gung-ho on his behalf."

"I curve balled my phone in a fit of fury." Dante pinched his lips, not wanting to reveal what happened between his epic curveball and his safe return. "Then Guy Lewis asked me to join the Bulldogs."

"Shit," Dad gasped again. "I didn't expect that."

Pop chuckled. "Still want to sue them, Liam?"

"Shut up, Hugo." Dad flicked on the video call, and his tanned features came into focus. Pops hovered behind him, as pale as beach sand. "So, why do I hear a but?"

"I met someone." Dante ran a hand over his face. "She hasn't asked me for anything, not even a date. I'm torn up, Dad. I...hoped, y'know."

Pops became all teary-eyed. "Oh, Liam, our boy's in love."

Dante waved a frantic hand. "No, no, it's not like that. It's lust. I'm pretty sure of that." He was still semi-hard, as if his cock expected another treat today.

"Ah-ha." Pop's white skin tone camouflaged his wide grin.

"Pops, I feel bereft like I lost out on an opportunity." Yes, that's what that feeling was, that sense of loss.

Pops nodded. "If you like her that much, then don't give up on her."

"Delaneys never quit." Dad furrowed his brow.

Dante rubbed his chest, running his thumb up and down his sternum. "She's a complicated ball of intrigue."

"And he's waxing poetic. Did you hit your head?" Dad chuckled. "Well, whatever you decide, we'd love to see you."

"I'll get away as soon as I can. Some South African sunshine is just what I need." And maybe he'd drag Pops into the sunlight too. "Love you."

"Ditto, my boy," they said in unison before hanging up.

Countless missed calls and text messages filled his notifications. He cleared them all. If it was urgent, they'd contact him again. He posted a smiling photo on all his social feeds. #alive #epic #adventure #chibougate

Then lay there, not sure what to do next.

He texted Jackson to let him know when Guy or his ex-teammates were ready to leave. Had he been able to bring his car, he would've been on his way home by now. The Ferrari didn't do rugged roads. Sipping his cold coffee, he browsed car websites to while away the time.

If he didn't quit on Fin, then he'd need an SUV.

Chapter Twelve

AN ACHING HEART NEEDED bacon and chocolate, but not together. Although, Fin angled her head, considering what fried bacon dipped in chocolate would taste like. That was her emotions talking, but it didn't matter. Not when she could be famous for inventing the best get-over-him food. She snorted. The odds of Dante seeing her splayed across the newspapers were minimal. Her then fatter ass would dominate the unkind photos. In the crowd, Bryce would be scowling, arms folded, a disapproving gaze on her too-wide-for-him hips.

Snapping the fridge shut, she swiped her dirty plate off the table and placed it next to the sink.

"You can't smother your sorrow with food, Finley." Her strangled voice pierced the silence of the cabin, a stark reminder of what lay in the future for her. No one to save her from the blues, or to talk sense into her when she considered smothering bacon with chocolate.

It wouldn't surprise her if someone had tried it. Mom had packed both, and Fin had consumed the stash. Her gluttony had spared her from her next gastronomical experiment. Queasiness churned what she'd eaten like her stomach protested the abuse. With a huff, she opened the kitchen cupboards, searching for something alcoholic, certain Alex had hidden a bottle somewhere.

He had clothes and condoms in *her* cabin, for pity's sake.

Condoms. Her breath hitched, and she hurried outside to raise her face to the crisp blue sky, sucking in great gulps of air. Dante had been in every room of the cabin. With his scent lingering, memories bombarded her. Angry at her stupidity, at the agony and hollowness consuming her chest, she paced, throwing her arms into the air as she muttered curses. What she'd suffered through with Bryce couldn't compare to her current emotional state. She'd caused this, brought this upon herself. What Bryce had done to her was all on him. That victim ship had sailed.

Stifling a sob, she burst into the cabin and opened every damn window, then stripped the bed. Holding her breath, she gathered the bedding and dragged it into the storeroom.

Tears trickled to her chin. She flicked them away, surprised she hadn't cried herself out yet. By now, Dante would be heading home. The chances of her seeing him again were as slim as a sexy man in uniform appearing at the front door of the cabin; sub-zero. Grabbing the ax, she stomped around the back to chop wood. Her actions were unforgivable in Dante's eyes, even though neither of them had discussed anything long-term.

She'd taken the decision out of his hands. That's what he would be pissed about. Still, if they met again by some random turn of events, seconds to disaster, she doubted he would greet her with open arms. She might have a pattern, love 'em and burn 'em before something deeper and truly remarkable blossomed.

What other choice had there been for her? Ending it now placed her in the exact place she needed to recover. Margot's afforded her the best in privacy, without Alex calling her a fool and Mom molly-coddling her.

No, a few days alone to grieve and to prepare for Russ's wedding was the best for her. *If* she could fit into her cocktail dress with the way she tried to smother her heartache with food. Thankfully, the cabin didn't have an oven, otherwise, cookies and cupcakes would be on the menu.

She didn't need the firewood, but the physical repetition of chopping soothed her. The midday sun stung her cheeks, and sweat drenched her vest to her body. Her shoulders blazed by the time her muscles trembled, weakened, and she almost dropped the ax. A decent pile of wood teetered, so she leaned the ax against the stump to gather an armload, carrying it inside to the storeroom. Nudging aside the bedding with her foot, she stacked the logs against the wall.

After several trips, she clipped the ax to the storeroom wall alongside the shotgun and opened the fridge for a soda. Its sweet, caffeinated goodness soothed her throat, and she peeled off her vest around the can in her hand. The air cooled the sweat on her skin, summoning a shiver and puckering her nipples. Grimacing, she tried to ignore the lust zinging through her, as if Dante hadn't this morning—

Biting her inner cheek to halt that thought, she slammed the can down and marched to the shower. She ducked under its spray. What she should do is focus on her writing, her next novel, and the promise to deliver the first draft to her publisher. She needed a happily-ever-after, something grand in gesture. And a name for her new series. Naughty Novelists? Seductive Scribes? She shook her head. None of those felt right. She'd need to give it more thought.

Rinsing the shampoo from her hair and checking no soap remained, she wrapped a towel around her and hurried to the radio. After a quick change in the channel, she unclipped the mic.

"Sugar Bear, this is Margot, come in." She tapped her fingers on the counter. Drying herself should've been her priority, but Patrick grounded her and had carried her through the darkest hours post-Bryce.

"What's up, baby plum? Over."

The sound of his voice calmed her, and she smiled, so grateful he'd answered. As her cousin, he knew which buttons to press. Calling her weird nicknames had started as an irritation but was now a sweet quirk.

"Just missing, you, little papa. Over." She sniggered. Two years older than her, he was by no means a father figure, but he ran a dojo. One drunken night, she'd spilled what Bryce had done to her, and her self-defense training had begun. It's why her next character would have some kick-ass skills. She would be a romance writer as well and suffering from a broken heart.

Like Fin's.

"Well, shucks, gosh darn it and roasted pumpkin. Come on by. Over."

She laughed. He'd made that up, mocking her galloping gorillas and leaping lizards. Her dad had said she had to lose her potty mouth for the clients. He ran a hiking tour business, not a bookie house.

The thought of spending the night drinking and laughing had far more appeal than her blank journal. Guilt struck her, cinching her chest, and she shook her head. Publisher deadlines suck. "Negative, twinkle tits, I got me a novel to write. Can do Friday night, if you're not too busy, y'know, drooling over strippers and the like. Over."

Alex had attended the bachelor party so teasing Patrick about more strippers was just for fun. As the only girl among her brother and cousins, she was far more relaxed around men, which was why Bryce's interest in her had taken her by surprise.

Dante's too.

"For you, my sweet, little starfish, I'm definitely free. I'll get the drinks, you get the pizza. Over."

She laughed. "Right, like the amount of pizza you consume won't bankrupt me. Over."

"And your choice of brandy isn't expensive? Can't wait to see you, Fin. Want a session before we overindulge? Over."

She stilled, her body still protesting the hours she spent chopping wood. "Yes, please. I'll hike from Margot's and meet you at the gate at sunset. Over."

"It's on. Until then, my spicy peppercorn. Out."

Chuckling, she meandered to the bedroom to pull on a clean nightshirt, then to the kitchen for a coffee. Snuggling into the unsexed lazy boy, she opened her journal with her pen gripped between her fingers.

Tessa, on the cusp of a divorce, fled to London on a business trip hoping to escape the horror of a failed marriage. Succumbing to an urge to dance, she headed for the club closest to the pub her colleagues had chosen. Self-doubt, along with three men intent on assault, hindered her night of dancing. Her training kicked in. She and the bouncer fought them off, but she received a knife wound in the process. Camden Mathews, the sexy club owner, distrusted her interference. Her sensual accent and sweet nature convinced him otherwise.

The sun set on Fin's cold coffee. Struggling to see the pages, she rose to close windows and light a fire and gaslights. Having stuffed herself on bacon and chocolate, she wasn't hungry. Hours blurred with fresh batches of coffee fueling her. If she could have a chapter or three ready for her publisher, it would buy her time to finish.

Too lazy to make her bed, she tugged a blanket off the back of the lazy boy and draped it over herself. Maybe by tomorrow, Dante's scent would no longer linger.

Chapter Thirteen

Dante pitched his famous curveball, and it smacked into the pitcher's mitt with power and accuracy. His arm and shoulder burned. He'd been at this since sunrise, unable to shake the discontent permeating his thoughts and plaguing his dreams.

Today was Friday. A week ago, he'd met a certain blonde bombshell. Four days ago, she'd abandoned him, not even asking his opinion on what they shared. Did it grate? Hell fucking yes. He gritted his teeth and pitched again. The thwack of the ball connecting with the mitt was a satisfactory reward.

Guy and a few Bulldogs players watched him from the dugout, but he long stopped listening to their praises. Yes, he was still a hose, his ISO score was good, batting average, slugging percentage... Their comments blurred, and in his current mood, he couldn't give a fuck what they said.

Signaling the batter he was done, he jogged toward the dugout, prepared to spin an excuse to his new coach. "Done for the day, if that's okay with you, Coach Ackerman?" He arched a brow at the mid-forties man, his bald head shining in the bright sunlight. "Off to pick up my suit for tonight."

"Sure thing, kid. With the way you pitch, we're sure to win the series. Hell," he laughed, which sounded like a wheezing smoker combined with a chainsaw, "maybe the next couple of series."

"Happy to be here." Dante hid his grimace by tucking his mitt under his arm and striding for the locker room. He threw himself against the wall of the player tunnel, grateful to the cool shade for hiding his mood. "Get a grip, Delaney."

But he couldn't shake the uneasiness.

"Duke?" A woman hurried toward him, her heels clacking on the concrete floor.

"Yes?" He forced a smile, not interested in chatting regardless of the delicious curve of her ass in those jeans.

"Missy Ramos, Baseball International." She held out her phone with its blue glow highlighting sections of her pretty face. "Do you have anything pre-signing to say?"

He forced a grin and bounced on his toes like Fin would do. Fire sliced across his heart at the idea that she influenced his behavior without being in his life. "Of course. I always have time for the press." He draped an arm across Missy's shoulders and steered her toward the locker room. "I'm excited to start this new chapter and with such an incredible team as the Bulldogs. Here, I'm not old, I'm one of the 'kids.'"

"How have your practices been so far?" She cast a sultry look with her lowered lashes over her big blue eyes. "You looked good from the bleachers."

Ice cinched his chest and froze his breath, like someone hitting him with a sledgehammer. He jerked to a halt and dropped his arm to splay his hand on the locker room door. What the fuck was wrong with him? "I was nervous about meeting such great players, but they made me feel part of their team and family. Now, if you'll excuse me, Missy, I have somewhere I need to be."

"I'll see you tonight at the party?" Her smile implied sensual delights, and pre-Fin, he would've snapped up the opportunity for a little fun. Now, his body didn't react to Missy's not-so-subtle promises.

He gritted his teeth and nodded, sliding into the locker room before she asked or implied anything else. Peeling off his uniform, he dumped it into the hamper and stepped under the spray, washing away the hours of sweat he'd earned.

Tomorrow, he'd return to Chibougate to talk to Eli and attend Russ's wedding. Was he a fool to see Fin again when she'd made it clear there was no chance? The air in his lungs expanded, filling him with overwhelming excitement. Yes, he wanted her to tell him to his face, to deny the chemistry between them.

Those liquid chocolate eyes, her sensual mouth, her ribbed abdomen... *Fuck.* He rubbed his bobbing cock that had minutes ago played dead. At least, he could deal with whatever this was and reset his system, so to speak.

Drying off, he hurried to dress in his jeans, white T-shirt, and brown leather jacket, dropping onto a bench to tug on his boots. Sliding his wallet into his back pocket, he flicked on his sunglasses and grabbed his car keys. In the player parking lot, his black Ferrari Portofino with red leather interior waited. He leapt in, not bothering to open the door. The SUV he'd ordered would arrive on Monday, too late for the wedding, which he hoped was reachable with his Ferrari.

As he roared along the outer ring road, he nudged his conscience, testing for lingering guilt. He'd lied about needing to collect his suit. That waited in a garment bag in his hotel room. He was in Ordmont, hours away from Anham and Fin. Becoming a Bulldog meant relocating to a new city and taking him farther away from Fin's beloved mountain.

He grimaced and whizzed into the underground car park, slipping his car into the first available bay. Powering off, he sat there, running his hands along the leather steering wheel as tension gripped his back muscles and spiked darts of pain up his neck.

His phone buzzed, and he pulled it from the glove compartment. "Dad." Just the man he wanted to speak to. "How are things?"

"Dante, I can't believe what just arrived." Dad's face appeared with his cheeks split wide. "This is an amazing gift. Why didn't you tell me you knew F.C. Margot?" He tilted the camera, and on his dining table sat Fin's book series.

"I…" Dante swallowed past the lump in his throat. One thing screamed at him; she'd thought of him. "I didn't ask her to do this, Dad. This is all on her."

"Wow, I can't believe you know her." A tear streaked down his father's cheek. "She addressed each one to me. See!" Dad pressed an opened book to the camera.

Dante frowned. "How did she get your address?"

"She sent a note with the books, said she googled me since you told her my first name. She assumed my last name matched yours." Dad wiped his cheeks with a chuckle. "All this effort for me."

"Love you, Dad. Glad you like it." Dante forced a grin. Shit, it was a surprise and indescribably sweet of Fin.

"When you see her, tell her how grateful I am."

"Will do, Dad."

"Night, my boy. Love you."

Dante stared at his phone, excitement once more consuming his chest like the crowd leaping to their feet at a home run. This intense emotion warred with the deep fear, dulling his hopes. He'd see her tomorrow and insinuate himself into her life. How she reacted to him showing up would tell him much. Had Russ mentioned to her he'd been invited to the wedding?

Fuck.

Resting his forehead on the wheel, he imagined Fin dancing, swirling her hips and shoulders. How he'd react was a given. Thumping the wheel, he leapt out of the car, pocketed the phone, and entered the elevator.

Once in his room, he raided his mini bar for little whiskey bottles then called down for something to eat. He planned on sprawling on the bed, maybe nap, or suffer through daytime shows, anything to keep his mind off his displaced thoughts.

Joy should be overwhelming him. After all, he had upgraded his team, would receive a pay increase and an extended contract. He emptied the first bottle and tossed it on the pillow beside him. Tugging out his phone and wallet, he placed both on the nightstand, yanked off his boots, and spread out on the bed.

After a quick set of the alarm in case he fell asleep, he flicked on the TV. There was no way he'd become drunk on two whiskeys, but drifting off was a possibility. He hadn't slept well since Sunday night with Fin in his arms.

Room service arrived, and he devoured the burger and fries, tasting neither. He drifted in and out of sleep as the afternoon ticked by. Too soon, he mingled with his new teammates, coach, Guy, and their plus-ones. The smile plastered on Dante's face was plastic. No one commented on his fake laugh or his lame jokes.

On his arm clung a blonde. Candace, Clarise, Charmaine, he couldn't remember. She was one of Guy's daughters, tasked to keep him happy and well-hydrated. She clung like a leech, her perfume too intense, and her voice grated, especially when she tossed her curls off her shoulder with a giggle.

Her breasts formed a cleavage carved by a master surgeon, and her tan glowed like her father's. Dante endured her company, for she kept others at bay. Missy had tried to part them, but C-something had dragged him away on a business ruse.

Posing for the press was as exhausting. C-something's hip felt wrong, too thin and unfamiliar. Draping his arm across her shoulders wasn't any different. Those weren't the shoulders he longed to curl into him.

At last, Guy hushed the crowd, with the reporters flashing their cameras and holding out their phones, eager to catch every word.

"In this envelope is your contract, finalized and ready for your signature, Duke." Guy beamed and held out a gold pen.

At the round of applause, Dante detached himself from C-something's octopus arms and accepted the pen from Guy. Leaning over the table, he scanned the contract, just to make sure it was as discussed.

He frowned. "There's no partial trade clause, Guy." Pinching his lips, he tried to understand the swell of contradicting emotions. Creeping through him was joy at the delay *and* frustration that they'd left his request out of the contract. He smiled at Guy and arched a brow, giving the man the benefit of the doubt.

"Yeah, about that—"

Dante's breath rushed out in a whoosh, and he held up his hand. "Not to be difficult for trade deadlines, but I had a reason to request it." He placed his palms on the table and over the contract. "It was my one stipulation, Guy. As I stand here, I see you have more thinking to do, whether you want to commit your time and energy to me, and whether the Bulldogs need me." He scooped up the pen and offered it to Guy. "Think about it, and let me know."

As he drove to the hotel, the millstone weighing him down lifted. Air rushed into his lungs, and he raised his chin for his temple to catch the wind over the windshield. He could breathe, and the relief coursing through his veins like cognac was warm and welcoming.

If Guy rejected his stipulation, Dante would accept that his life had changed course. For once, he was content to let the Fates decide his future.

Chapter Fourteen

Fin set out for the gate just after two on Friday afternoon. The hike would take about three to four hours, depending on her pace and any obstacles en route. Her journal was all she'd packed in a spare bear bag that thumped her back with every step she took. Pinecones and needles softened the ground beneath her boots, adding a spring to her movements. She meandered the winding path heading south and away from Margot's. Vincent Falls lay east of the cabin, but she followed the curve of the mountain to the edge of their property where she'd meet Patrick.

"Breathe, Fin, Patrick will wait. There's no need to rush."

She sighed and forced herself to slow her steps. Climbing over exposed roots and clearing boulders off the path helped. Taking a break at each obstruction kept her in the moment. Grimacing at the tepid water in her bottle, she lifted her face to the sunlight, hoping for a cool breeze to dry the sweat dewing her skin. The sharp scent of pine filled her nose along with the rich aroma of soil from the stones she'd relocated. Small abrasions on her fingertips remained as evidence she'd struggled with too-large rocks.

Surviving the last few days had been easier if she hadn't thought past the now. No thoughts went to what she would wear tomorrow to the wedding, what she'd have for dinner, or what Patrick would put her through during their training session. No, only now mattered, keeping her longing for Dante at bay.

She twisted her lips and capped the bottle, cursing her stupidity. "Focus on the pine needles, Fin, on the dark brown tree bark, on the patches of wild mint growing in the forest's shade. One step after the other."

Distracting herself hadn't helped, nor had her splintered heart healed. Cocooning in the cabin and away from any media had given her a sense of bravado. But as she returned to the real world, someone was bound to mention Dante.

"Look at the sun's rays filtering through the canopy, idiot."

She gritted her teeth and marched onward. The descent flattened, and the pine trees thinned. Patrick waited a hundred yards ahead at the gates of Chibougate. He'd endured much as rebellious Russ's older brother. Both had the McFarlan looks: dirty blond hair and warm brown eyes.

Patrick rested his ass on his white jeep's fender, crossing his denim-encased, long legs at the ankles. "Hey, Ms. Daisy." He bounded across the distance between them with ease.

"Hey, cousin." She returned his hug then thumped him on the shoulder when he swept her off the ground and swung her like a sack of corn. "You'd swear you haven't seen me in months."

After climbing in the passenger side, she dropped the bear bag at her feet. *Climbing* being the operative word. Sure, Patrick and Russ were tall, Alex too, so it was a mystery where she got her short stature. Mom denied Fin was adopted, but family lied to each other all the time.

"I don't feel like training, Patrickster." She rubbed her palms along her camo-encased thighs. "How about we eat pizza and drink ourselves into a stupor?"

"Y'know, we're not teenagers anymore, my feisty ferret. I've got to do adulting things tomorrow."

She winced and rested her temple on the cool glass. "True."

He careened his jeep along the dirt roads, heading for his home on the outskirts of Kearmack.

"What's going on, Fin? You're not your usual self." He arched a dark-blond brow and reached across to squeeze her hand. "You look the same as—" He pinched his lips. "Has Bryce contacted you?"

"Hell, no. And he better not." She forced a smile. "I have a lot on my mind, daddy bear."

"I know that expression, baby spice. Got anything to do with that baseball player Uncle Eli mentioned?"

Ice burst across her face, but she blamed the air conditioning rather than thoughts of Dante thrust upon her again. She shook her head, tossing her curls wild. Mother of pearl, how to deceive her beloved cousin...

"Nah, my last novel put me through the wringer." It had, so it wasn't a complete lie, despite her twitching eyebrow.

He snuck a glance. "Why? You love to write."

She shrugged. "It's a new series. The first book is super important."

"What's it about?"

It was sweet of him to ask, and as her dearest cousin, he did so because he cared about her. She doubted he'd read one of her novels, though, and she wouldn't ask him to. Just the thought that he, Russ, or Alex, shit, even Dad, read her erotic romances spread wildfire through her system. No, *nein*, *het*, and hell no.

"A romance author writes about a romance author finding love who writes about a romance author finding love." She shrugged. "I'm breaking the fourth wall."

He chuckled. "That's pretty cool."

"I thought so too. Tessa gets herself involved in a brawl. I'll need you to make sure I spell the Krav Maga techniques correctly." Fin threw up her hand, halting him mid-speak. "Relax, I'll text you the word, and you can confirm its spelling." She laughed. "The way you guys react, you'd think I'd asked for a sperm donation."

He laughed as he spun the steering wheel gripped with confidence in his long-fingered hands. "Firstly, as your cousin, that's never going to happen; mixed genetics and all that. Secondly, I've read your books, sweet cheeks."

What the cuss? No, he hadn't said what she thought he had. He had to be pulling her leg and threatening to give her a heart attack. She gaped, twisting in the seat to face him. "Bullspit."

"Honest to goodness, and cross my heart." He fake-punched her on the chin. "Got to support family, Fin, y'know that."

"I'm stunned, scared shitless, and so happy." She sucked in a sharp breath, trying to calm the suicidal moths in her stomach. "How were they?" Chewing on her lip, she refused to blink, not wanting to miss his expressions. Patrick would never lie to her, so how he reacted would be authentic.

"Epic! I thoroughly enjoyed them, especially the naughty bits." He winked. "The whole damn town's proud of you."

"What?" Heat burned across her sun-kissed cheeks as if she sat too close to a bonfire. "The townsfolk know?"

He chuckled. "Best kept secret."

"Oh, galloping gorillas, Patrick. Pastor Harris knows I write erotic romance?" She buried her face in her hands, which muffled her wails. "Not Mrs. Grosvenor, my grade three teacher?"

Patrick chuckled. "Yup, there's even an FMC Book Club dedicated to reading and rNoellewing your releases. Aunt Noelle makes sure they get copies a week or two in advance."

Fin squealed, throwing out her hands like she had to stop an impending collision. "Mom knows they know and didn't tell me?"

Mortification barreled over her. Now, every time she went to town, everyone, except the tweens and babes, had read her novels. And like Patrick had said, all the naughty bits too. Her stomach lurched, trying to toss its contents. She pinned a hand to her mouth and blinked at her laughing ass of a cousin. How dare he find humor in this?

She groaned. "I'm never leaving my cabin again."

He jerked his jeep onto the tarred road, fish-tailing its ass. "Quit your complaining. Tonight, we feast and make merry."

"Is everything prepared as requested, James?" She opted for a subject change and added a posh accent, but she planned to harass him for info when next she wrote a sex scene. Maybe getting him to reveal sex from his perspective would put a permanent blush on his cheeks. Hell, she might even add him to the acknowledgments.

"Of course, ma'am."

She widened her eyes, impressed with his fake British accent.

He flicked at hand at the road. "We're stopping at Big Al's for the pizza, then heading home. Need anything?"

"Nope, just pizza." She curled into the seat and rested her cheek on the headrest to stare at him. "How do you feel about tomorrow? Ready to gain another brother?"

"Russ and Carl have been dating for years." Patrick grinned. "And the best is, Russ is moving in with Carl again. This past week has been insane."

She gasped. "Shit, will Russ be joining us?" As much as she adored her younger cousin, she wanted to be selfish and hog Patrick for the evening. He understood her better than anyone in her family.

"Nope, Alex has whisked him away for drinks and a pre-wedding dinner. As long as we keep to my apartment, Russ won't bother us when he creeps in at who knows what time." Patrick pulled his jeep to a halt outside Big Al's and twisted to kiss her temple. "But I warn you, my little piñata, no strippers and no hooking me up with any barmaids."

She laughed. "Damn, I'll have to message Candy and Cindy not to show." Folding her arms across her chest, she harrumphed. "You're costing me a pretty penny, Mr. McFarlan."

He chuckled and opened his door.

"I'll hide here if you don't mind, Patrick."

He paused, studied her flushed face, then nodded. "Sure thing, honey." Meeting her gaze, his expression turned serious. "No one's judging you, Fin. The bible does have the Songs of Solomon and breasts like prancing gazelles. Own your success, Fin. You've earned it."

With her chest expanding, burning with joy, she watched him bound into the pizza house. Shit, she loved how supportive he was and how wonderful he made her feel. A tear slipped past her defenses, and she rolled her shoulder to capture it. No matter who she met, fell in love with, had her heart ripped out by, and her ultimately ending up as a Botticelli spinster, she had Patrick to see her through it all.

She wasn't alone.

Chapter Fifteen

DANTE LEFT AT EIGHT on Saturday morning with his phone silent. Having not heard anything regarding his contract, he packed his things and checked out of the hotel, just in case. The drive to Anham would take a few hours, then another hour to Kearmack, the town closest to Chibougate Tours. He would have plenty of time to poke his heart to figure out what the hell was wrong with him.

At each refuel, at each stretching of his legs, he tried to ignore the growing excitement inside him. Soon, he'd see his jellybean. What he wanted to say to her tumbled through his mind, jumbled thoughts merging between anger, frustration, and this urge to sweet-talk her into dating him.

His breath caught, and he gripped then released the steering wheel, increasing the Ferrari's speed to reach her sooner. He was a little over the limit, but he didn't care, willing to pay whatever fine if the highway patrol stopped him. Sighing, he tamped down on the gas, slowing enough not to find himself inside a jail cell. That would just delay him.

As he crossed the boundary into Kearmack close to midday, his stomach did a flip flop, and he broke out in a fine sweat. Purring the Ferrari along the main road, he admired the colorful awnings shielding the quaint shops from the bright late-fall sunlight. Flower boxes lined the sidewalks, and folks strolled about with coffee cups in hand.

He grinned, tempted to search for movie cameras filming the too-idyllic scenery.

A cop waved him down, forcing him to pull over. Frowning, he did as instructed. He hadn't been speeding, had stopped at the sign and the pedestrian crossing.

"Good day, Sheriff Moore." Dante read the cop's name off his badge.

"Hey, Duke, surprised to see you back in Kearmack." Moore circled Dante's car. "Nice!" He paused alongside the driver's side. "There's no way you can drive this to Chibougate. Park it by the station, and I'll take you with the cruiser."

Dante tried to hide his shock. How did the cop know where he was headed? "Thanks, Sheriff, appreciate it." He'd hoped the road would be drivable, but it wasn't surprising that his Ferrari wouldn't make it. The trip to the police station was minutes away, and he parked beside the sheriff's cruiser. Hopping out of his car, he pulled his luggage from the trunk and climbed into the passenger side.

"Russ mentioned he invited you. Didn't think you'd pitch, though." The sheriff pulled off with a broad smile. "The town's bouncing with excitement. Carl and Russ are high school sweethearts, y'know."

"No, I didn't know that." Dante hadn't pegged Russ as gay, but then again, their interaction had been limited to the helicopter's headsets. "I'm looking forward to it, and I'm also hoping to discuss business with Eli."

"Sounds promising. You're cutting it fine, though. The ceremony starts in little under an hour."

Dante shrugged. "Drove from Ordmont."

"Whoa, quite a trip." Sheriff snuck a glance at him. "How does your car handle?"

"Want to take her for a spin, Sheriff?" Dante grinned. Lifting his ass to tug his keys out of his back pocket, he dropped them into the center console.

"You'd let me?" Sheriff Moore tightened his grip on the steering wheel.

"Sure, my thanks for the ride." Then Dante swallowed his tongue as they drove into the Chibougate parking lot. He curled his fingers into his palms to hide their trembling.

"I'm sure Eli and Noelle have a cabin for you. Ask reception to radio me when you're ready to head out of Kearmack." The sheriff pulled into a parking bay in front of the paved walkway leading to the reception cabin.

Dante hesitated, then nodded, slid out of the cruiser, and grabbed his luggage.

The thump of the driver's door said the sheriff followed.

Strolling toward the cabin, he tried to keep his stride steady when his pounding heart deafened his ears. His palms slicked with sweat, and he almost dropped his bag. Sucking in a deep breath, he opened the door.

The moment he saw Fin, he knew he was in trouble. A week apart had done nothing to reduce the chemistry between them. Faced with her in an evening gown, his starved eyes feasted on the baby-blue creation. Diaphanous frilly bits spiraled down her body, enhancing parts he'd fondled, kissed, or sucked. The top of her breasts rose and fell with her ragged breathing soothing his concerns that she wouldn't be happy to see him.

Hope had swept across her cherubic face, sparkling her eyes and spreading her sensual lips.

Then a cloud of sadness descended, wiping away her instinctive reaction. Fear lingered in her warm cocoa eyes. His heart thumped in response, radiating a burning agony outward. The urge to cross the reception to sweep her into his arms gripped him, but her stiff shoulders warned caution.

FIN STARED AT DANTE'S picture in the newspaper where a statuesque blonde clung to him, her body language a little too sensual for Fin's liking. She stroked his smiling face, wishing it was her he held against his chest. The suit he wore hugged his broad shoulders, and his crisp white shirt parted, exposing the caramel skin of his throat. Her lips tingled in memory of the kisses she'd pressed there. Like an addict, withdrawal pangs twisted her insides.

Popping painkillers against the lingering hangover, she folded the newspaper, not covering his face but hiding the woman. If she hid him, someone might read more into her actions. Hiding the blonde might lead to teasing Fin that she was jealous. That was preferable to suggestions she'd lost her heart. With a shuddering sigh, she rose to her feet, slapping the folded sports section on her thigh.

Her dad had one more meeting before they could head for the wedding. Her mom was at the church, helping with the final arrangements and leaving Fin to man the reception desk.

"What's the hold-up, Dad?" She wiggled a foot in a navy pump. "I don't want to torture my toes longer than I need to." The poor dears were beginning to feel like sardines in a tin can.

"Then why wear them, Finny?" Dad raised his chin, asking her to tie his bowtie.

She did, huffing at his silly question. Centering his tie, she smoothed his lapels and neatened his kerchief poking out of the pocket. He looked suave in a tux.

"I need the extra height, they make my calves look good, and hiking boots don't match."

"Mom said no to the hiking boots, didn't she?" He grinned, squeezing her forearm.

Fin huffed. "It's not like I plan on meeting my forever-man at the wedding, not with my family circling like judgmental buzzards."

Studying himself in the reflection of a framed painting, Dad adjusted the bowtie like she couldn't center it to save her ass. "Sam's coming."

"Sam is free to leave uncontested." She folded her arms across her chest. "I'm not budging on this, Dad, so quit throwing him at me."

"He's in love with you, Finny. Have mercy on his heart."

"I am, by letting him know from the start that I'm not interested. Now quit it." The front door opened, ending this pointless conversation. She was tempted to roll her eyes at her father. Instead, she pasted on her professional face, the one she wore when a patient claimed he had no idea how a fidget spinner got stuck on his dick.

Her breath caught. Partially obscured by shadow, Dante hovered in the doorway. She beamed. Hope bloomed in her chest, rippling goosebumps along her arms. But he couldn't be here. It made no sense. Her silly heart had to stop this torment.

She slumped, wishing she didn't see him in every man crossing her path. "Hi, welcome to Chibougate." She lowered her gaze to the reservation book. All the guests had arrived. Frowning, she flicked the page over. Maybe Mom had written it somewhere else? Or was this visitor who Dad was waiting for?

"Hi, jellybean."

That voice! Ice engulfed her face, sending her vision into a spiral, and she snapped up her head to gape at him. "Dante?"

The ice traveled to her toes and weakened her knees. Gripping the counter kept her from fainting. Right, woman hits floor. How cliché, but knowing her luck, she'd hit her head on the way down and lose her memory.

"Hey, Duke. You're right on time." Dad gestured to him to come into his office.

Dante obeyed, lowering his luggage beside the desk as he passed her. His gaze lingered on her face, but she couldn't read his expression.

When the office door closed, panic gripped her, sent shivers across her skin, and churned nausea in her stomach. Her receding hangover rose to ping behind her eyes, and yet a drink was exactly what she needed.

She grabbed her phone, planning on texting Patrick for a rescue, but put it down before she succumbed. A Clarke was made of sturdier stuff. She could survive whatever this was. Wobbling on her heels, she scurried across to pin her ear to the office door. She tried to discern words. Instead, it was a mumble-mumble peppered with their laughter. What could they be discussing?

"Um, Finny, should you be doing that?"

She squeaked and leapt a foot off the ground, spinning to face the sheriff. Heat rippled from her cheeks to her neck, and she kept her chin to her chest. He could sniff a lie a mile away. She wanted to blurt out that not a drop of liquor had crossed her lips, nor had she kissed two boys behind the school shed.

"Ready for the wedding, Uncle Tim?" She sidled away from the office door, trying to look innocent. Needing to keep her hands busy, she grabbed the newspaper to unfold.

"Sure thing. I'm on duty, so in my uniform, it'll have to be. Maria's dressed to the nines." He chuckled, leaning his ass on the arm of the couch. How this great lummox had landed the town's beauty queen, Maria, was a story worth telling. "The whole town's all fancy-like."

"Carl and Russ's wedding has been a long time coming." It was a struggle to focus on a non-Dante-related conversation. Accepting she'd been caught red-handed, she hooked her thumb at the office. "Know what that's about?"

"Nope, and it's none of my business. Closed doors imply privacy needed." Uncle Tim grinned. "So, what do you have against the man, Finny?"

She gasped and paused in the middle of smoothing the newspaper creases with her palm. "Nothing."

"Yeah," he smirked, "and you used to be a better liar."

She slumped, fighting the fiery agony of a broken heart that she'd managed to hide by sheer will. "I'm not... He's not... It's complicated."

"I see that." Uncle Tim unfolded his arms as the office door opened.

"Welcome, Dante. Fin, issue cabin nine to our newest business partner."

"What?" she yelped.

Dad had his arm thrown across Dante's shoulders. The man who'd stolen her heart stared at her with a dark intensity in his eyes. His pulse ticked at the base of his jaw, and the air around him promised...retribution, pleasure? She couldn't decide. Either one had her heart leaping, dancing, then doing a bungee dive into her stomach.

"Oh, hi, Tim." Dad slipped past Dante and the desk to speak to the sheriff.

Fin didn't follow him, instead, she gaped at Dante. "What are you doing?"

"I bought into Chibougate as I planned to before our...adventure."

She shuddered, unable to fight off his deep and sexy voice stroking her skin. "Right." Refolding the newspaper, she hid his face and slid her thumb along the crease, now displaying the model. Dante's gaze rested on the article before flicking up to meet hers.

The front door opened, and a man entered with a confidence she recognized.

"What the fuck...?" she whispered, staring at Bryce, fear settling like an iceberg in the marrow of her bones. No, it couldn't be.

"Hello, Finley."

Nausea rose to choke her and lodged in her throat. She croaked his name, amazed she could speak through the fear paralyzing her. So much for her kick-butt lessons. Typical. When she needed herself to be strong, she went all damsel-like.

"This is Bryce?" Dante stood beside her. She hadn't seen him move. The warmth of his body and his spicy cologne shredded her heart but quietened the fear.

"Yes." She squeezed the word out, then released a sigh. "What are you doing here, Bryce?"

"You've been gone long enough, Finley. It's time to come home." The once-suave doctor waltzed deeper into the room, his sweet smile nauseating.

"Leave. Here. Now." She circled the desk, squeezing past Dante, who blocked Bryce's path to her.

Dante touched her elbow, and she paused, meeting his gaze. She rested her fingers on his chest, long enough to pat him. She had this was what she conveyed, but who knew if he understood her.

Bryce's bright smile didn't affect her like it used to. "Enough with this nonsense, Finley. You know I love you."

Love? That did it. In a blaze of retribution, the fear disintegrated, giving way to furious anger. "Bullspit. Love isn't demeaning me or hitting me, and it sure as shit, isn't doing the local anesthetist under everyone's noses." She laughed, hating every inch of his salon-tanned face, his dark hair, his dark-blue eyes, the slight kink to his nose, and that horrible mustache he now sported. "Leave."

"The lady has asked you to leave." Dante warmed her back, his protection breathtaking.

"Who is this, Finny?" Dad's shoulders stiffened.

She smiled, no longer concerned about the doctor she'd thought she had loved. "No one, Dad."

Bryce bristled. "Listen here, you bi—"

A crack reverberated through the room.

"Dammit." Dante shook his hand, pain twisting his sensual lips. Blood dribbled to his fingertips. She hurried to gather his hand in hers, assessing the skin split over his knuckles, the swelling and bruises forming.

"Why did you do a fool thing like that? Your hand is worth more than a million, moron." She snapped her gaze to his. This close to him, the gray flecks in his blue eyes almost glowed.

A slow smile curled his lips. "I didn't know you cared, Fin."

"I'll sue your ass." Bryce cupped his jaw, but he released it to grab her arm, squeezing a yelp out of her.

"Release me, Bryce. This is your final warning." She widened her stance, balancing her weight on the front foot.

"Or what? You're getting in the car, Finley. I'm not asking you again." He tugged, but she didn't budge. Patrick had taught her how to be sturdier on her feet, with or without heels.

With a wild laugh, she was unable to still the excitement bouncing her on her toes. "So glad you still don't listen to me." She stroked his shoulder to lure him to relax his grip.

He did, nodding at her as if he'd won.

She yanked him toward her, pulling him off balance and into her rising knee. Two groin shots later, he bowled over, exposing his nape. With a hammerfist to the back of his neck, he fell to his knees, then collapsed on the wooden floorboards. He curled into a ball, howling in agony.

"Go ahead and arrest him, Uncle Tim." She flicked a glance at the sheriff. "After the last time he hit me, I filed a restraining order against him."

Facing the witnesses, she enjoyed their stunned expressions. Dad and Uncle Tim grinned, pride widening their smiles and twinkling their eyes. Dante's surprise was in his gaped mouth, but his hooded gaze and flaring nostrils were so sensual her nipples tightened.

To hide her reaction, she kneeled beside Bryce to speak in his ear. "I can hit back, Bryce, but my self-defense isn't as good as my shotgun skills. Violate the restraining order again, I won't hesitate to use it."

Uncle Tim hoisted her up, placing her beside Dad before helping a whining Bryce to his feet. She wiggled her fingers in a wave as Bryce limped out of the cabin.

"Patrick taught me that, Dad. What do you think?"

"I'm so proud of you, sweetheart. But soon, we'll discuss why you had to learn self-defense in the first place, Finny." He leveled his no-nonsense gaze on her. "Now, I'm heading to the church. See you two there?"

She grimaced but nodded. It was naïve of her not to tell her family why she left Anham, a promising career, and the supposed love of her life. "I'll rush Dan...Duke to the Emergency, then rendezvous afterward."

Dad kissed her temple, smiled at Dante, and left.

Dante hovered, cradling his hand.

Shit. She bit her lip. He smelled so good. Shaking her head to dispel his mesmerizing presence, she fetched the Bronco's keys and ushered him through the door. "Right, let's get that looked at."

Chapter Sixteen

DANTE'S KNUCKLES BURNED LIKE the fires of hell, but he didn't care. Hearing the fear in her voice when she croaked Bryce's name was enough of an incentive to beat the living shit out of the man.

Proud of Fin, Dante's chest swelled like an expanding balloon filling with helium.

He shouldn't have bothered, not with the way she'd brought Bryce down. *Fuck.* He'd never seen anything so damn sexy. Studying his hand, he flexed it, testing the pain. Nothing burned like it would if broken.

"I didn't know you were invited." She didn't look at him, smile, or welcome him as he hoped she would.

He sighed. "Yeah, Russ asked me on the helicopter ride over."

She rolled her bottom lip across her teeth but said no more. Her shoulders stiffened, telling him she didn't want to discuss her betrayal, though, he doubted she saw it that way.

"How have you been, Fin?" The Bronco was no place for the conversation he wanted to have.

He needed access to her, her body, those sweet, enticing lips of hers, the curve of her neck, and Lord willing, a bed nearby. No matter how he shifted his ass, he couldn't ease the hard-on he sported. Her perfume filled the Bronco's cabin, tormenting him and threatening to decimate his control.

"Fine." She closed her eyes for a moment before focusing on the road. "You?"

"I missed you." Shit, he hadn't meant to say that.

She gasped and snuck a glance at him.

Jerking the Bronco to a stop at the hospital, she leapt out and hurried around the hood to open his door. He wasn't useless, but he let her help him.

"Let's hope the x-ray machine is working." She hurried ahead to keep the automated doors open. "Gladys, we have a hand injury here. Not sure if anything's broken."

An elderly nurse crossed the antiquated but clean reception to lead him into an adjoining room. "What happened, Finny?"

"He fought for my honor, Gladys." Fin clutched her fist to her chest in an over-dramatic gesture and fluttered her eyelashes. "He's my hero."

"Quit your antics." But Gladys snickered as she positioned his hand on the x-ray table before she and Fin ducked behind a shield. A few clicks later, she gestured to the two of them to wait outside. "I'll develop these and see if Dr. Steinberg can assess them now."

Fin held the door open for Dante, and he sat on a plastic-covered chair while they waited. Fin chose to pace, looking goddess-like in her figure-hugging evening gown. With his tongue, he wanted to trail where those frilly bits brushed her body, then follow the same path with her naked.

"Gladys will dress your injury when she returns." Fin wrung her hands as she paced.

"I don't think anything's broken, jellybean. We'll make it to the wedding."

She stilled, and the pain-filled gaze she settled on him pierced his heart like a blazing arrow. He rose to his feet, cupping her elbow to draw her close.

"Good news, it's not broken." Gladys nudged her head, asking him to follow.

He hesitated, pressed his lips to Fin's temple, and trailed the nurse.

It didn't take long. Gladys administered a pain shot, cleaned his shredded knuckles, bandaged his hand, then slipped on a sling to minimize movement.

"No more defending Finny's honor, hero." She winked as she ushered him out of the consultation room.

"I can't make that promise."

She studied him for a second, then nodded. "Good luck, Duke."

He grimaced. Did everyone know who he was? He sighed at that silly question. As the only celebrity in town, what did he expect? Striding toward Fin, his chest expanded again, filling with tingles, butterflies, and warmth.

"All good?" She studied his sling, then flicked a glance at Gladys. "Thanks." Slipping her arm around his waist, Fin ushered him to the Bronco. Unable to resist the temptation, he draped his arm across her shoulders, pulling her into the curve of his body.

"I have to change for the wedding, Fin."

She stumbled and raised a wide-eyed gaze to meet his. Then she nodded, pulling away to open the passenger door for him. "We'll pick up your luggage from reception and get you settled in your new cabin." She slammed his door and darted around the hood before climbing into the driver's seat. "Shouldn't take too long. We can slip in and sit in the back pews."

The ride to Chibougate was in silence.

He twisted in his seat to watch her, which didn't help her relax. The sunlight caught her curls, and they shimmered, glowed, looking so soft that his good hand twitched to touch them. She wore dusky pink lipstick that matched her skin tone to perfection, but she chewed on her bottom lip. He longed to do that, to test the plumpness of her lips with his tongue, to delve into her sweet depths.

"Quit staring." She flicked a glance at him. "You're making me nervous."

"Just nervous?" His voice was like gravel, but he didn't clear his throat. He wanted her to know how she affected him.

She jerked the Bronco to a halt, left the engine running, and jogged into the reception, returning with his luggage. How she could move with ease on those shoes, he couldn't say.

"Right, almost there." With his luggage behind her seat, she drove them around the reception cabin to number nine.

He trailed her inside the cabin, which looked much like the one he'd used after she'd abandoned him. If this was his, he wanted touches of Margot, similar lazy boys too.

She dumped his luggage and garment bag on the bed and turned to leave.

"Um, Fin, I need help."

She squeaked, froze, then faced him. "With?"

"Buttons, zips, that sort of thing."

Her sensual mouth parted on an 'oh,' and she ran her gaze up and down his body, making him fully hard. He didn't try to hide it from her, and judging by the pink on her cheeks, she noticed.

"Right." She drew in a deep breath and marched across to him, determination in the tightness of her jaw.

Within seconds, his sling and T-shirt were off. Her nails scraping his skin made him hiss. After unzipping his garment bag, she unhooked his white shirt, then slid it with care over his hand but yanked it over his other arm, revealing a little of her frustration. She wanted this done and as fast as possible. Her focus was intense as she buttoned his shirt. Nibbling on her lip wasn't helping his hard-on subside. And this close, he could breathe her in. The way her perfume clung to her skin was an aphrodisiac.

Toeing off her pumps, she kneeled and removed his polished black shoes. When her fingers fumbled with his belt, a wave of need barreled through him. He almost gripped her hips to toss her on the bed, the wedding and his injured hand be damned. She tugged his belt free, then unzipped him like his jeans were a duffle bag.

"Grab my suit pants. I'll shimmy out of these." He didn't need her inches away from a full-blown erection.

She dived into his garment bag like it would save her. He smothered a chuckle while he struggled with one hand to pull his jeans off. Her gasp raised his gaze to meet her hot chocolate eyes. Desire pooled in their liquid depths before she dropped her chin to her chest.

Kneeling in front of him, she held a pant leg for him until she could pull it up. As soon as she yanked his pants in place, she slid his belt through the loops. "Shirt in or out?" She met his gaze again and froze, her mouth parting for her tongue to moisten her lips. "Fuck, Dante, decide."

Decide? Oh, he had. It was she who needed to choose. "In."

Pinching her lips, she tucked his shirt in, nudging his cock again. Her fingers trembled when she zipped him closed, brushing his hard-on as she did so. He groaned, raising his face to the wooden beams, sucking in sharp breaths. He swallowed his growl when she buckled his belt tight. After slipping on his shoes, she pulled a chair closer, climbed onto it, then opened his suit jacket for him to slide in.

"This is the same suit as in the newspaper article?" Her words were soft but her accusation clear.

He grinned, enjoying her unexpected jealousy. "Yes, I wore it for about an hour last night."

Her breath hitched, and she jerked back as if he'd slapped her.

He captured her cheek, holding her still. "When Guy omitted the trade-in clause from my contract, I left the party *alone* and spent the night watching TV in my hotel room, jellybean."

Her skin warmed under his touch. He stroked his thumb across her lips, wishing he could kiss her now. If he did so, they wouldn't make it to Russ's wedding, and she wanted to be there for him.

"Ready?" Her rasping voice was sex-on-a-stick sexy.

He closed his eyes, unable to bear the temptation. "Cologne and comb."

She pulled away from him, dug in his luggage, and held up his bottle of cologne. Halfway to him, she uncapped and sniffed it, her eyes stuttering closed on a blissful sigh. "I've always liked the way you smell."

Surprised at her revelation, she squeezed her eyes shut on a small moan, then thrust the bottle into his good hand. Finding the comb took longer, and he wouldn't tell her it was in a side pocket, wanting to watch her ass wiggle while she emptied his luggage. As he'd determined, he was a masochist.

"Yes!" She thrust the comb into the air like she'd found treasure.

He chuckled and ran it through his hair, bending his knees to look in the gilded mirror.

"Ready now?" She toed on her pumps and hurried to the door, assuming his answer was a given.

"Could you release one or two buttons? The shirt is choking me."

She huffed and tapped her toes, waiting for him to bend to her height. While she unbuttoned his shirt, he slipped his arms around her, pulling her snug against him.

"Have I told you how beautiful you look, jellybean?"

She gasped, her fingers stilled, then splayed over his chest. Her hot touch scorched him through the Egyptian cotton.

"You have no idea how much I want to kiss you, do you, Fin?" He studied the expressions flitting across her eyes. She was drowning in a sea of turmoil. Lust parted her lips in anticipation, heat burned her cheeks with embarrassment, yet what stopped him from going for the kill was the doubt and fear darkening the cocoa brown of her eyes.

"The sling?" He released her, gripping her hip to steady her when she swayed.

"Right." She stood there for a second, her breathing harsh and her fingers on her cheeks. Then she burst into motion, slipped him into the sling, and hurried to the Bronco.

He sighed, closed the cabin door behind them, and strolled to where she held the Bronco's door for him. Tonight, he needed this resolved, or she'd be the death of him.

Chapter Seventeen

Fin couldn't breathe, not with Mr. Smells-so-good in the Bronco with her, not with his sensual words repeating in her mind, watering the cracks in her soul, and healing her heart. No, she didn't care that he'd gone home alone and hadn't done the horizontal tango with the model.

Liar.

She winced. Now she couldn't even lie to herself.

How would she survive tonight, tomorrow, or however long he stayed? As a business partner, cabin nine was his forever. Two doors down from her cabin put him too close for comfort. Shit, there went her ability to sleep. Maybe she could sweet-talk Patrick to escort her to Margot's? Running? Hell, yes. What else could she do?

Slipping into the church, he rested his good hand on her hip, his touch possessive. It sent thrills of excitement and happiness through her. She wanted to sob, to hide, to run. Couldn't he see how returning only broke her heart? Why couldn't he just stay away?

They sat in the back pew, his arm draped around her like they were a couple. If she wiggled away, he followed and made it worse by pressing the length of his thigh along hers.

She tried to focus on the kaleidoscope of colors the sunlight streamed through the stained-glass windows. Uncle Tim stood out in his uniform, and his wife looked stunning in her dark-green cocktail dress. Dad and Mom were in the front pew, and Patrick's messy hair was visible above the guests' heads.

Russ in a tux faced Carl, whose Italian good looks contrasted with his white suit.

Pastor Harris addressed the church, his deep voice reaching to the farthest corners of the little church. "We are gathered here—"

"Russ looks happy," Dante whispered in her ear, his breath brushing her earlobe.

The shiver it summoned puckered her nipples, and she hurried to fold her arms across her chest. He didn't need to see how he aroused her.

"Carl too and so elegant in white." She tilted her head to Dante. Not realizing how close he was, she brushed her lips across his. Smothering her gasp, she closed her eyes as mortification burned fire along her veins.

"Do that again."

She met his gaze, bowled over by matching desperation in his cobalt eyes. The need trembling his body mimicked her own. Drawing courage around her, she plucked at his bottom lip with her own. His breath hitched, and he gripped her knee, keeping her close.

This was insane. She was playing with fire.

"I love your mouth." His words puffed across her lips, tempting her to toss her inhibitions to the side. Then he claimed her with a hot kiss, spicy and so masculine that she leaned into him, almost begging him to deepen it.

He didn't. Instead, he released her and nudged her chin to face forward.

"We have much to discuss, jellybean."

She nodded but couldn't think about what. He scattered her thoughts, and with his body warming hers, his arm possessive, she cherished the moment. No matter what the future brought, she was happy here and now with him.

When Russ and Carl hurried down the aisle arm-in-arm, she leapt to her feet to kiss them. Was it over so quickly? Patrick, as the best man, swept her into his arms, crushing her in a hug. He carried her around the pew before lowering her, now that there was space for his antics.

He thumped Dante on his shoulder. "Welcome, Duke. I'm Patrick, Russ's brother."

Dante grinned, fluttering her heart. Holy mackerel, the man should be outlawed. She smothered a hysterical giggle as she imagined petitioning Uncle Tim to brand Dante as wanted, dangerous, and too sexy for any sane woman.

Dante shook Russ's hand. "I see the resemblance."

"Yeah, well, I can't help that I got the good looks in the family." Patrick shrugged. "How are you feeling, my mini pompom?"

"A tad hungover. You delivered, big daddy." And he had. All that pizza had dissolved in pools of brandy. She swallowed, ignoring the nausea rising at the thought of melted cheese.

"And then some." He rose on his toes, searching the crowd. "Take good care of her, Duke. I've got adulting things to do."

She held out her hand to Dante, which he accepted with his good hand and without hesitation. Her heart leapt at how easy it was to resume what they'd started at Margot's. Releasing her hand, he looped his arm around her waist and tugged her against him. She didn't say anything, just watched the townsfolk stream past, eager to toss biodegradable confetti on the married couple.

"So, is it broken?" Dad asked as soon as he was within speaking distance. Mom trailed him, lingering to chat to a few townsfolk with bright laughter twinkling her eyes.

"Nope, but I'll happily do it again."

Fin gasped at Dante's words.

Dad studied Dante, flicked a gaze at Fin, then grinned. "Looks like you have a champion, my girl."

"Not that she needs one." Dante kissed her temple. "It was so damn sexy when you took him down, jellybean."

She blushed, shooting a glance at Dad, worried that he'd heard Dante's whisper.

"I didn't know she could do that," he said to her father.

"Neither did I." Dad pinched his lips, and a frown marred his brow.

"It's lovely to see you again, Duke." Mom smiled, joining them. "And welcome to the Chibougate family."

"Thank you, Mrs. Clarke." His intense gaze snagged Fin's, implying something she couldn't understand.

Mom waved a dismissive hand. "Enough of that, call me Noelle."

He nodded. "If you call me Dante."

Fin squeaked but didn't dare speak her thoughts. Giving out his real name meant one thing, a future here at Chibougate. Yes, he had bought into their business, but that didn't mean he'd be a permanent fixture. Shit, she was moving to Margot's with no hope of ever coming down from the mountain.

"Duke's a nickname, and I don't want Fin having to watch what she calls me when we're not alone."

She blinked at him. Oh, no, leaping lizards, he didn't just announce to her folks that they were *seeing* each other.

"Dante it is." Mom winked at Fin, shooting heat to the tips of her ears.

"The way my little girl is blushing, Dante's Inferno comes to mind." Dad chuckled.

Fin groaned. "Dad."

Without another word, Dad escorted Mom toward the church's large wooden doors.

Spinning on her heels, Fin jabbed a finger at Dante's chest. "Quit it. We're not an item, there is no 'us,' and stop touching me like you have the right."

"You're so sexy when you're angry." His husky drawl drew a squeal from her.

She thumped him in the exact spot she'd jabbed him.

"We're going to have a discussion, jellybean, about why you chose not to pursue what's between us and why you used the helicopter to prevent our relationship from deepening."

She frowned. Yes, she'd done that.

He gestured between them with his fingers. "There is an 'us,' we *are* an item, and not touching you is like not breathing." He gathered her against him, ignoring her thumps to his chest and her wiggles to escape him. "You're lucky I don't throw you over my shoulder and toss you onto my bed." He growled, "And stop wiggling, dammit. I only have so much control."

She stilled, her breathing ragged. "I don't appreciate your highhandedness."

"Neither did I appreciate yours." He dipped his head, forcing her to meet his gaze. "Talk to me, Fin."

She pinched her brow, trying to hold back the words barreling up her throat. "You overwhelm me, Dante. I can't think when I'm around you. I want your touch, your kisses, your deep and slow fucks, like I'm some sort of an addict." Dragging her gaze to meet his, she studied his expressions, hoping to understand just one. In for a penny and all that. "I...can't have my heart broken again, y'see. I wouldn't survive. Breaking this off, and again now, is the safest for me."

"Safe?" Suffering, pain, and sadness hardened his laugh. "Safe isn't crossing that damn river. Safe isn't taking chances with wild bears and poachers. You risk your life every day, Fin, why not risk your heart with me?"

Time stilled as she blinked at him, memorizing every curve, angle, and texture of his face. Fire burned her chest, and she released a breath on a whoosh. "What are you saying, Dante?"

His smile was gentle, yet tremulous, as if he feared rejection. In his eyes was his heart, all that she made him feel. "I'm in love with you, jellybean."

Like a crescendo, a tidal wave, a volcanic eruption, joy, excitement, and love churned from her gut, rising to overwhelm her heart and bring on the tears.

"You love me?" Emotions strangled her voice. She shook her head, swiping at the spilled tears. "No, it's not possible." Her vision spun, and she threw out a hand to catch the back of the pew. Instead, Dante caught her hand and pulled her into the curve of his body.

He loved her.

"What's not possible? You don't believe I can find you beautiful, adorable, stubborn, reckless, sensual, caring, pragmatic, and considerate? Woman, I'm barely keeping it together being this close to you. Why can't you see it if Eli and Patrick can?"

"No, I mean…I tried not to love you, tried not to hope, not to yearn for what-ifs and maybes. I wanted to forget you, Dante." She cupped his cheek, admiring his beloved face. "I'm not a model, but a park ranger, for pity's sake. You're famous, Mr. Big-time-baseball-player."

"You're not famous too, F.C. Margot?" He chuckled, kissing her temple, her nose before feathering the gentlest of kisses across her lips. "I planned on pursuing an 'us,' but what gave me hope you returned my affection was the gift you sent my dad. Jellybean, that told me you still thought of me." He burrowed his face into the curve of her neck, his lips brushing her skin, sparking tingles along her nerves. "Now, let's go to the reception. The quicker we start the evening, the sooner I can make love to you."

She moaned, eagerness warring with her sense of duty. Dante making love to her was more than she dreamed of. "Wait. Don't you want to know how I feel?"

A slow sensual smile spread across his lips. "I know you love me, Fin."

She gasped, digging her heels in the church's parquet flooring, preparing to whack him upside the head.

"You wouldn't have chased me away if you didn't. You would have had a meaningless affair with me and waited for it to peter out."

"Oh." Tears spilled free again, putting her waterproof mascara to the test.

He captured her chin between forefinger and thumb, his touch gentle yet firm. His gaze was unwavering as he brushed his mouth across hers. "Now, come, my love. Russ said the way you dance is something to behold."

"What?" She broke his grip to press her fingers to her cheeks. "That's only when I'm drunk."

Dante laughed. "Then let's get some champagne into you."

Staring at the man who professed his love was like facing the brightest sunlight and letting it warm every dark inch of her. She smiled and accepted his offered hand. "Are you trying to get me drunk, Mr. Delaney?"

"No, I'm just trying to get you, Ms. Clarke, anyway I can."

Her breath caught, and she leaned into him, splaying her hands across his chest and sliding her fingers inside his jacket. "Well, you've got me. Now what?"

He slanted his mouth across hers again, so warm and masterful, curling her toes in her pumps. She groaned, clinging to him as he slipped his tongue past her lips, flicking it, teasing her, and snatching her ability to breathe.

Her heart thumped in her ears, and his heated cologne bombarded her senses. When he broke the kiss, she trembled with need.

"You're my weakness, Dante."

He grinned and brushed her hair off her temple before delivering a sweet kiss to her cheek. "Good."

Chapter Eighteen

THREE GLASSES OF CHAMPAGNE later, Fin gyrated her body like a stripper. Dante grimaced, despite being unable to look away. His cock throbbed, making demands he was eager to fulfill. Could they leave now? The dinner, toasts, and first dance had happened, and he'd greeted the entire townsfolks individually.

Rising to his feet, he prowled the dance floor, nearing his prey. At his touch, she twirled into his arms like a ballerina, with laughter in her dancing eyes and wearing her sweet smile. She swayed her hips to the hypnotic beat, rubbing against a part of him that needed no more stimulation.

He hissed, and she stilled, raising a wide gaze to his.

"Are you in pain?"

He nodded, and that was that. She laced her fingers through his and dragged him around to bid everyone good night. The cool evening air washed across his face when they left the hall. He drew in a deep breath, thankful for the little calm it restored to him.

Ignorant of his suffering, she ushered him into the Bronco before driving to his cabin. She helped him inside, yet the moment she crossed his threshold, he flicked off his sling, banged the door shut, and pinned her to it.

Gripping her ass, he slid her up the door to meet his descending kiss. She tilted her head and deepened it from the start, dueling his tongue with slashes of her own. Breathing became inconsequential, and where her body touched his, he burned.

"I missed you too." Her four words slammed into him, and he spun, carrying her to the bed.

She lay there, her dark gaze admiring as he stripped off his jacket and shirt, popping the buttons in his haste. Then she unbuckled his belt and slid down the zipper.

It was his undoing.

Spots circled his vision, and he struggled to breathe.

Cool air brushed his cock. He blinked at his pants and boy shorts pooled around his ankles. She stroked his thighs, cupping his balls, drawing a bone-deep shudder from him.

He leapt out of her reach to toe off his shoes, shake off his clothing, then grabbed her heels, spreading her legs wide. Bright pink panties peeked out. He tossed each pump, slid his hands down her calves and under her knees to her thighs.

"Your hand, Dante."

"It's fine." He kneeled between her hips, gripped her ass, and lifted her onto his lap. Running his fingers from her outer thighs to her hips and up along her waist, he searched for the zip at her side. Finding it was an eureka moment, filled with elation. He chuckled, then nipped the mounds of her breasts and nuzzled her nipples through the soft fabric while he unzipped her.

The dress parted, and he hooked a finger under it to glide it off her, kissing each inch of exposed skin until her nipples popped free. His heartbeat stilled, then raced ahead. He groaned, dipping his head to capture one into his mouth. Lust and love drove him, and he was too far gone to be gentle.

She cried out, curving into him. Her nails dug into his back, shredding the last of his control. He tumbled off the bed, taking the dress with him. Fin in a pink G-string was the stuff of wet dreams.

"Jellybean, you're so fucking beautiful." He tugged on the thin silk, peeling it off her body.

She raised her hips to help him, shoving her sex into his face. Groaning, he tossed the G-string and feathered kisses up her inner thigh, flicking his tongue between her feminine folds before trailing a wet path up her stomach.

Capturing her mouth with his, he nestled his cock at her entrance, trembling at the restraint he used not to plunge into her wet depths. Then she looped her legs around his hips, and he slid in an inch. A growl slipped through his gritted teeth.

He pushed off her. "Let me do the fucking, Fin. My control is non-existent."

She smiled, and his breath stilled. Love for him poured from her gaze, spiraling around his heart and expanding it. "There's no need to hold back. Show me how much you missed me, my love."

He cupped her cheek and brushed a thumb across her bottom lip. "I love you, jellybean."

"I know." She raised her hips, and he slid in another inch.

He succumbed and slammed into her, arching his back and grunting at the sweet heat of her gripping his length. She whimpered, writhing beneath him even as her nails grazed his taut nipples. Now that he was seated, he leaned back and slid his fingers between them, rubbing her drenched nub. Her eyes flew wide, and she cried out, gyrating her hips as she climbed toward her release. Each twitch, each hip swirl, rubbed his cock. Tingles skittered from his balls to his head, warning that his orgasm was imminent.

She screamed his name and came apart in his arms. He'd never seen anything more beautiful. Her channel squeezed him with tiny spasms, and he withdrew to thrust in again. Her mouth parted on an 'oh,' and he repeated, hoping to get the same reaction. She clung to his arms and rubbed her nipples across his. Then she stilled, and heat gushed across him. It was too much, too intense, and he splintered. He held himself in place, looping an arm around her while his hips pinned her.

Wave after wave of pleasure washed over him. He couldn't speak; his jaw clenched on the sensations loving her added to his orgasm.

She slumped, taking him with her to the bed. He sprawled across her, shivering where their skin touched. Gathering her across him, he rolled to the side. Their breathing merged, loud in the silence of the cabin.

Resting her head on her open palm, she twirled a pattern around his nipple. "When do you leave?"

"Depending on whether Guy amends the contract, maybe never."

"Just like that, give up what you love?" She sat up. "Why does the trade-in clause matter so much?"

"Most contracts insist the player relocate to the team's home base. But I needed Kearmack to be a drive away, Fin."

"Kearmack?" Her eyes shimmered with tears. "You knew then?"

"That I loved you?" He smiled, capturing an escaped tear with his thumb. "I suspected." He sat up too, needing to snatch a kiss. "I have at the most, ten years left in my baseball career, and not agreeing to the trade-in clause raises my hackles. If they truly wanted me, it would be a non-issue. Maybe it's time I chose a different life."

"No, you're not giving it up for me. What if you grow to hate me for it?" She shook her head, capturing his hand to kiss his palm.

"This is the feeling I had the day I met you, sweetheart. This isn't on you."

"I can follow you, Dante, live in whatever city you choose."

His heart burst, and he blinked back the tears. She'd give up Chibougate? He kissed her, yanking her onto his lap as he tried to convey how much she meant to him.

"We're often on road trips. I'd prefer for you to stay with family than weeks alone." He crushed her against him, thrilling in her silky skin against his. "If Guy signs it, then we'll discuss it." He smiled, nuzzling his chin in her curls. "Now that I'm here, how about we hike up to Vincent Falls and enjoy what it has to offer."

"What? It will be freezing."

He brushed his palm over her nipple, fascinated when it puckered under his touch. "I'll keep you warm."

She spread her legs, straddling him, and pressed her body to his. "You better." With a kiss to his chin, she stroked his throat and along his shoulders.

"I'll keep you warm for as long as I live, jellybean." He groaned when she flicked her tongue across his nipple.

She shared her warm smile with him, her heart and soul in her warm cocoa eyes. "You better."

About the Author

Sevannah Storm is a fiction writer who immerses herself in fantastical worlds both magical and science fiction. She has a flare for the creative, having studied art and interior architecture, and spends her time drawing, oil painting, and writing. An avid reader from an early age, Sevannah finds her inspiration from various sources: games, novels, music, and the land of make-believe. The unique versus the practical has brought on numerous debates.

In her spare time, she does Pilates and rereads novels that snatch her breath away. Having embraced the social media world, you can find her on most platforms.

Her home is a land south of Wakanda, where animals roam free. Born in Zimbabwe, she grew up in South Africa. The crisp blue skies with cotton-candy sunsets expand her heart and soul, encapsulating a sense of freedom.

Words she lives by: "Know your pothole and dodge it. Don't work in a pencil factory if you're a vampire."

Sevannah loves to hear from her readers. You can find and connect with her at the links below.

Website/Newsletter:

https://www.sevannahstorm.com/

Facebook:

https://www.facebook.com/sevannah.storm

Instagram:

https://www.instagram.com/sevannah.storm/

Twitter:

https://twitter.com/sevannah_storm

Thank you for taking the time to read *Loving Finley*. If you enjoyed the story, please tell your friends and leave a review. Reviews support authors and ensure they continue to bring readers books to love and enjoy.